HUNTED

INTERSTELLAR BRIDES® PROGRAM: BOOK 17

GRACE GOODWIN

GET A FREE BOOK!

JOIN MY MAILING LIST TO BE THE FIRST TO KNOW OF NEW RELEASES, FREE BOOKS, SPECIAL PRICES AND OTHER AUTHOR GIVEAWAYS.

http://freescifiromance.com

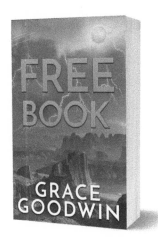

INTERSTELLAR BRIDES® PROGRAM

YOUR mate is out there. Take the test today and discover your perfect match. Are you ready for a sexy alien mate (or two)?

VOLUNTEER NOW!

interstellarbridesprogram.com

1

*V*ice *Admiral Niobe, Interstellar Brides Testing Center, The Colony*

"Run. You know I like the chase. I will catch you and then..."

The male's deep voice was a rough whisper, but I heard it across the vast space between us like he was right beside me. He didn't need to finish his sentence. I knew what he would do when he caught me. It made my skin prickle with awareness, my pussy clench with need.

I was fast.

He was faster.

I was cunning.

He was ruthless.

I was a Hunter.

I was also the hunted.

I was his prey. His desire. *His mate.*

And when he found me, he'd take me. Command me. Fill me. Fuck me and make me his. Completely.

I wasn't running from him because I didn't want him.

I was running because I did.

My heart pounded not because I was tired, but because I was excited. Eager.

And so I ran faster, for the hunt was part of the mating. I would not allow a male to claim me who was not worthy. And he would not claim me if I didn't test him.

The terrain was steep, the trees thick, the canopy of leaves overhead blocked out much of the sunlight. The air was damp, warm. Almost sultry.

I smiled as I quickly pivoted around a large tree, leaped over a fallen log.

"You're wet for me. I scent your pussy from here."

I whimpered because it was true. I was slick and needy. I wasn't just overheated from the chase, from the miles we'd covered. I was desperate for his cock. He moved so quickly, his footsteps were light upon the ground. Yet I heard him as easily as he did me. His breathing was shallow, sweat dampened his skin. I breathed him in, would recognize the dark scent anywhere. Anytime, for the rest of my life.

Most females would stop. Wait. Let her mate catch her. Gods, most females wouldn't run to begin with. But I wasn't most females. I was Everian. A Hunter in my own right. A warrior. And so I moved even faster. The ground was a blur beneath my feet, my hair blew back from my face from the pace.

"When I get you beneath me, mate," he growled, "you will know who you belong to. Who owns your pussy.

You'll come when I say. On my cock. Beneath my mouth."

The thought of his head between my thighs, his tongue on my clit, swirling and teasing that swollen bud, distracted me. I stumbled but didn't fall.

"Ah, mate. You want my mouth on you?" He'd heard the falter in my steps. "Then let me catch you."

I laughed, narrowed my eyes as I burst into a clearing. "Never."

When I heard him groan, my heart leapt with joy. He wanted my fight. My spirit. My need to prove my strength before I submitted. Because I would. I would revel beneath his dominance. His strength. For while I might give over to him, I held the power over him.

My thoughts had distracted me, for all was silent. No footfall, no chase. Only the animals of the forest, the wind. He was no longer chasing.

His tactic changed. I slowed, then stopped when all remained silent.

Turning on my heel, I looked in all directions. Searched. Listened. *Felt.*

I heard it again.

Heartbeat.

Breath.

Inhaled what belonged to only him.

Dark scent.

I spun on my heel and there he was. Before me. I had to tilt my head back to meet his heated gaze.

"How—"

He grinned, the smile feral and yet sweet.

"It matters not, mate." His chest expanded as he took a deep breath.

That rankled. I would not be bested so easily. I fled.

He laughed.

He caught me again. I had no idea how he did it, but I couldn't discern his location until he was upon me. Like a cloak, shielding him. Hiding his movements.

I didn't know this skill. It showed, for all at once I was grabbed, spun about and pressed into a tree. He touched me as if I were made of glass, even with the aggression that pumped through our veins.

"Submit," he growled.

His hand was on my waist, the other on the tree beside my head. His full length pressed into me. Every hard inch of him. I felt his cock, the thick length against my belly.

I was torn. The power of the mating was dividing my focus. I wanted to bolt. To run. To be chased once again. More. I needed the exhilaration of it. But I craved the feel of him. His heat. His hardness.

I wanted to fall to my knees before him. I wanted to strip myself bare, lie back on the grass and part my thighs.

I wanted to get upon all fours, look over my shoulder and watch as he mounted me. Claimed me. Took me roughly, just as I needed.

A large hand came to my chin, tipping my face up to his. "Say it. Say the one word that will make you mine."

I swallowed, then licked my lips. He was here. He'd found me. Hunted me. There was nothing else I could do, *wanted* to do.

"Yes."

He dropped to his knees before me, tugged the boots from my feet, the pants from my body so I was bare from the waist down. He was as swift in this as he was in chasing me. In an instant, my legs were over his shoulders and his mouth was on me. There.

His body pressed me into the tree. I was elevated, off the ground with no purchase, nothing to grip but his head, my fingers tangling in his hair. He licked into me, parting me. Finding my clit, circling it.

A primitive sound rumbled from his chest as he pushed me into orgasm. I knew I dripped onto his face, I was so eager, the climax so intense.

"Why?" I asked when I could catch my breath. He didn't move his head as he kissed the inside of my thigh, but only lifted his eyes to meet mine.

"Why am I kneeling before you when it is you who will submit?"

I nodded, my back bumping against the rough bark.

"Your body, your pleasure, is mine. *You* are mine. While I might be the one on my knees, you're giving me everything."

I couldn't see the thick outline of his cock, but I knew it was hard. Eager to fuck.

"What about you?"

In a flash, I was laid upon the soft ground, my legs still thrown over his shoulders.

He shifted to open his pants, pull out his cock, to align himself to my entrance and thrust deep.

"Yes!" I cried at the fullness. The feel of him in me. Stretching me. Claiming me.

"There's the word again. Your consent. Your submission."

He pulled out and I whimpered, but I was upon my hands and knees with him mounting me from one blink to the next. He took me then. Deep. Hard.

His strong body curved over my back, his mouth at my neck, nipping at my racing pulse, biting at the juncture of my neck and shoulder. "Mine."

I gripped the damp ground for purchase, but there was none. He moved us across the forest floor, the sounds of our skin slapping together, the wet slide of his cock in and out of my pussy all that could be heard. We'd scared the animals away.

We were the animals. Wild and frantic. He rutted into me and I cried out, ready to come again.

"Such a greedy pussy. So wet. Perfect for me. *You're* perfect for me. Mine."

"Yes."

"Give it to me."

I knew what he was talking about. Not just my orgasm, but my body. My soul.

My inner walls clenched him like a fist, pulling him in, wanting him, needing every thick inch of him.

I screamed as I came, the sound echoing across the forest, over the land where he'd hunted me.

He thrust deep. Tensed. Groaned. Came. I felt the heat of his seed as it filled me, as it made me his.

And he was mine, for while he was the dominant one, I had given him the ultimate pleasure. He would not be complete without me.

And I... I submitted to it all. Willingly. Happily. Completely.

My eyes flew open and I gasped.

"No!" I shouted, the single word echoing off the walls of the bare room.

"That good, huh?"

I blinked, looking up at Kira's smug face. My friend leaned over me, but hopped back when I sat up abruptly.

I rubbed my hand over my eyes. Gods, that had been intense. So real. But it had all been a dream. A stupid bride testing dream.

Rachel, another Earth woman who'd been mated to the governor of The Colony, remained silent, but the corner of her mouth was tipped up. Yeah, she was internally laughing.

Doctor Surnen, who was in charge of all testing on the planet, held his tablet from the other side of the testing chair. I wasn't sure if he was quiet because he knew the testing involved intense sex dreams or because I was the first female he'd tested and he wasn't sure what to say to me. From what I'd been told, I was currently the only unmated female on the planet besides the mother of another Earth mate, Kristin. This doctor did not normally test females. He only tested integrated fighters who were transferred here after they'd escaped captivity.

I knew my nipples were hard, but I definitely wasn't sharing that with the doctor. I didn't have a hard on because I didn't have a cock, but my pussy ached for the sex I'd vividly imagined... but hadn't had.

I was horny. Hornier than I'd ever been in my life. Was the testing supposed to be cruel, to get you all hot and bothered with no chance of relief? Was it so that the person being tested would be so desperate to come that they always approved the match just to get guaranteed sex?

At this point, with those traitorous nipples and my pussy clenching for a cock to fill it, I'd probably approve a match to a planet whose males were blue and had two penises.

"I came here to visit you and Angh, not to be tested," I reminded, not for the first time.

She rolled her eyes. "You did both. A very successful trip."

I climbed from the testing chair and stretched. Bad idea since it only rubbed my nipples across my Academy uniform. I whimpered.

Rachel laughed.

"I don't like you," I grumbled and gave her my head-of-the-Academy evil eye which usually had cadets peeing in their paints. She only laughed harder.

2

ℰlite Hunter Quinn, Latiri 4, Hive Integration Base, Sector 437

HEAVY MANACLES CIRCLED MY WRISTS AND NECK, MY DRIED blood the only sign of what the Integration units were trying to do to me.

Make me one of them.

Hive.

Control me. Control my strength and my hunting skills. Control my mind.

I would die before I gave in to the buzzing noise inside my skull. The sound grew louder with each round of injections. I lost more of my mind, even as I felt my body growing stronger.

I'd watched two lifelong friends, two Elite Hunters like myself, die writhing in their cells. But they had not turned into the enemy. They had fought to the end, and they'd denied the Hive what they wanted. More fighters. Elite warriors.

My brothers had not given the blue Hive bastard running the base what he wanted. I was the last of us. The last Elite Hunter in these underground cells. His last chance to succeed.

The others had fought him to the end. As would I.

"I see you are awake, Hunter." The dark blue alien was a patchwork of silver and dark, vibrant blue. His eyes were nearly black. Completely opaque, there was nothing behind the orbs, no shine of emotion, no soul. Not the blue of a bright sky, something darker and far more sinister. I knew I faced the infamous Nexus, one of the mythical leaders—or creators—of the Hive systems. My information came directly from the I.C., the Coalition Fleet's Intelligence Core. Fewer than a handful had ever been seen, and only by human females from a new Coalition planet called Earth.

"What do you want? I don't go for men, and I don't go blue, so don't get too excited." The Nexus narrowed his eyes at me but showed no other reaction. But he knew what I meant. I could sense his irritation in the air.

"I have no wish to breed with you."

"Thank the gods for small favors."

That irked him further. "You make attempts at humor, Hunter, but they will not save you. You will be mine in the end."

I shook my head and stared into his eyes. The act made the noise inside my head increase to a roar, the pain like needles boring into my eyes, but I held that gaze and dared him to kill me. "No. I will be one more dead warrior, and you will be a failure."

The Nexus snarled, raised his hand and struck me across the cheek.

The Nexus were not like their drones. They reacted. They referred to themselves in the first person, not the third. They were *alive.* They were individuals.

They could be manipulated. Frightened.

Taunted.

I smiled at the blue creature even as he lifted his hand to signal one of his drones to begin another round of injections. The needles pierced my neck and wrists, burrowing deep, pumping my body full of microscopic Hive tech, nanocytes so small the doctors in the Coalition had no hope of ever removing them from contaminated warriors like me. Were I to survive, my hunting days would probably be over. Depending on the extent of the integrations, I could be banished to The Colony, useless and forgotten.

There was no hope for me, but I kept the smile on my face as the Nexus walked away. When he was gone, I sank back to sit against the wall. They'd left my uniform on when they'd captured me but taken my weapons. The suit kept my body temperature regulated for comfort but could do nothing to protect my mind from the stark reality of this cave. This entire base. The transport station within view of my cell. I saw new captives arrive by the dozens: Prillon, Viken and human, Atlan and Xerimian— although few of the latter two—too dangerous to seize in large numbers. Fewer still were the Everian Hunters, like me. The fact that the Nexus was running an integration facility right here, on this planet, right under Commander Karter's nose, was beyond scary. Insane, even. No one knew we were here. *Right* here where they weren't looking for us because it was assumed it was Hive free.

The thought brought fury, and the adrenaline coursing through my body cranked up the volume in my head once more. I couldn't afford emotion. I had to be calm if I was going to fight the Hive tech and keep my sanity, if I was going to win this war with the blue fucker who intended to break me.

Taking a deep breath, I slowed my heart rate and imagined my scarred friend Zee and his new mate back on Everis, living a peaceful, happy life. If Zee were lucky, he'd have two or three young ones running around each day, and his beautiful Earthen mate, Helen, would surrender to his touch each night.

I'd hoped for a female of my own, a tender, submissive female who would need a strong hand to both comfort and pleasure her. I'd even gone in to the Interstellar Brides' Program and taken the matching test, followed their protocols. That had been months ago. No mate had arrived to share my life, no female had been matched to me. Perhaps I was too broken. Too scarred within. Too full of rage. I knew I was no longer a fit male, and still, I'd clung to hope. But staring into the cold, black eyes of the predator Nexus for the last few days, I allowed the hope for a mate to die along with the rest of them. I didn't need hope, not here. I needed strength. Defiance. Determination. Will.

The Nexus would not break me. He might kill me, but he would not break me.

———

Kira came over and hugged me, which made me stiffen in surprise. "Yes, you do," she said. We might have worked together at the Academy, and secretly on missions for I.C., but that didn't mean I wanted her to squeeze me. "It's over. Like a shot when we were kids. The thought of it was worse than the actual jab. Wasn't the testing good?"

She wasn't giving up goading me, for the question was followed by a wink.

"You know my stance on having a mate. I'm thirty-six years old. I've made it this far without one, so it seems silly now."

"Yet you got in that chair on your own. We didn't force you," Rachel finally said.

She was right. I hated her, too. I sighed. I'd been required to take leave from the Academy, but I had no family to visit. Even though I was half Everian and had lived on the planet for two years before joining the Coalition, I didn't feel like I belonged there. I would never go to one of the outer planets for a vacation, and I wouldn't have come to The Colony if Kira hadn't invited me. She'd done so more than once and I'd given in—not because I didn't like her but because I didn't like not working—which had landed me in this stupid testing chair. I hadn't been drunk; I could drink the largest Atlan under the table due to my mother's Russian heritage and my predilection for vodka—which seemed to be in my DNA.

What wasn't in my DNA was a desire for children. A family. Anything a Coalition mate would expect out of a bride. I might have a uterus, but it wasn't open for any kind of business. Not a chance.

"I know," I replied, running my hands down my uniform, smoothing wrinkles that didn't exist. They hadn't forced me to be tested, but I'd done so without any excitement. Who would I get? I was half-Human, half-Everian. I had never fit in on Earth growing up and I was the Earth-chick on Everis. I was, as usual, odd. I didn't like to be out of sorts, out of control, and all I felt was ruffled, sweaty and mussed as if I'd just had sex. But I hadn't. God, who was that couple I'd dreamed about? *That* had been a relationship. Intense. The connection had been incredible. But the way the female had submitted to her mate? Yeah, that didn't work for me. I submitted to no one. I was a vice admiral in charge of the entire Coalition Academy. I didn't need a male to boss me around.

I could certainly use his cock, though. *That* could definitely boss me around, especially the way the guy in the dream had given it to her. God, yes. But a cock without a male was just a dildo, and I had plenty of those.

"You're not required to make babies," Kira reminded, as if she'd been able to read my mind. Or she'd listened to my constant grumbling about *why* I shouldn't be a bride ever since she and Rachel suggested it.

"You both did," I countered, looking between the women. I didn't have tons of friends because at the Academy, I had to remain separate from the students and most of the staff. I was in charge and I couldn't just pal around.

These two women had taken me under their wing during my visit, even when I hadn't been too thrilled about it. They knew I was prickly and often times annoying by my ability to solely see things in black and white—not literally but figuratively. But they were from Earth and it had been great to talk Earth things. Hair dryers. Real ice cream made with dairy from a cow, an animal that existed only on Earth. I hadn't felt quite so... different.

Somehow, they'd cornered me about remaining single all this time. I was six Coalition deployments past the time to be tested and mated. I was an old maid and I'd been fine with that.

"We're not you," Kira replied. "We wanted to make babies."

Duh.

"Dr. Surnen, tell the vice admiral how she's not required to birth lots of alien babies for her mate," Kira said.

The doctor, who moved to sit in a wheeled chair, glanced my way. "The vice admiral doesn't need this repeated," he said. "I won't insult her intelligence."

Smart Prillon.

I smiled and nodded at the male.

"Fine," Kira grumbled. "Then I will. You're smart, but you've got your head up your ass about this. The testing matches you to *your* perfect mate. That means if you don't want a baby, then the testing knows that. It won't match you to a guy who wants twelve kids. It's your *perfect* match."

I glanced at the doctor, who nodded.

"Well, it's not like a match happens right away," I said, heading for the door to the testing room that was part of the medical unit. "I'll go back to the Academy and I can wait. I've heard from some of the warriors here that they've been waiting for years."

The doctor cleared his throat and we all looked his way. "I'm sorry to disappoint you, Vice Admiral, but you've been matched."

My mouth fell open. My heart dropped into my stomach. "What?"

Kristen and Rachel both giggled and clapped their hands like cheerleaders at a pep rally. Why did I like them?

"You've been matched."

"I heard you the first time," I grumbled at the doctor. "What does that mean?"

"It means you've been matched to Everis and to an Elite Hunter."

"Of course, you're matched to Everis," Kristen said. "Makes sense since you're half Everian and you've got a mark."

I flipped my hand over and stared at the mark on my palm. Growing up on Earth, I'd thought it was just a birthmark. But when I'd gone to Everis, I'd known it was so much more. To others. To me, it didn't mean anything. I wasn't holding out hope for a marked mate, obviously, since I'd just been tested. And matched. "I didn't even know I was half-Everian until those Hunters found me on Earth when I was fourteen. To me, having my mark awaken would be like magic, and I don't believe in that. No, I'm not a romantic holding out for that kind of stuff. I'm... realistic."

Rachel cocked her head to the side and gave me a soft look. "Realistic? I'll say. I've seen you in the Pit."

I'd gone with them to watch the fighting matches, but

had volunteered to participate. It wasn't often they had Hunters fight. And a female.

"Please, I can only imagine what people in high school said. Varsity track, right?"

I hadn't been lying when I said I hadn't known I wasn't all human. I'd just thought I was odd. So did everyone else where I'd grown up in Minnesota, especially after my mother died and I'd ended up in foster care. The orphan who did normally impossible things. When I was little, I could hear conversations I wasn't supposed to, and that had gotten me in lots of trouble. I thought back to that not-so-fun time of my life when I was older, after I'd learned to hear but keep quiet, when I'd been ridiculously fast, crazy ruthless and never knew why.

All of a sudden, I felt everything I had back then. Alienation, insecurity, anger. I'd been the rebel, like the goth chick who wore tons of black eyeliner just to piss people off. I hadn't worn *any* eyeliner, but I'd known how she felt. I'd been the star athlete at a huge school, because I'd broken all state track and field and cross-country records, making me a hero at school. I could have won nationals, easily, but I held myself back because I'd been barely winded. My heart rate had hardly gone up, even after a five-mile run. I hadn't wanted the glory. I didn't want track scholarships to college, where I would have to try to figure out just how much I could show of my abilities without drawing too much attention. I didn't care about Ivy League schools or the Olympics. I missed my mom. I don't remember much of her, her smile, her scent, her voice, but I missed the *feel* of her. God, her hugs. I was alone in the world, and the only one who accepted me was dead.

I didn't want attention. I wanted answers. I'd wanted to know why I was a freak.

I knew *now*. I had Everian blood in me. I had no idea how my mother had gotten it on with an Everian in Minnesota, but she had. Had my sperm donor gone back to Everis after a quick fuck on Earth? Had he been killed? I'd never know. Hell, if those Everians hadn't been on Earth to hunt and read about my championship running win, I'd probably still be on Earth. It wasn't as if they'd given me a choice to remain once they saw my mark, saw me run like the wind. I'd been forced to return with them to Everis, to be Everian. Which, while in my DNA, wasn't easy. Talk about culture shock.

"There's no way I'm going to Everis now to live happily ever after with my mate," I told them, and glanced at the doctor to make sure he knew I was serious. "My duty is to the Academy. I have no plans to retire."

"You don't have to, but you *do* have to go to him," he said. "You two can work out the details after..."

I arched a brow and crossed my arms over my chest. "*I* have to go to *him*? I'm headed back to the Academy tomorrow. He can transport and meet me there."

"It's tradition. I'm sorry. The bride who is tested is always transported to the male. You would dishonor him if you refused."

I frowned. "I'm not going to get into the reasons why that *tradition* should be changed."

"Do you wish to reject your match? Dishonor him?"

Damn it all to hell. That was the last thing I wanted to do to an honorable warrior. "No. I do not."

"Excellent." The doctor held up his hands as if to block my verbal assault. "You will transport to him. What the two of you decide, where you will live, is completely up to you."

"You can wear the pants in the family," Kira told me with a wink. "Just go to him."

I rolled my eyes. Growled even. The truth was I'd *loved* that testing dream. Every moment. I didn't want to wear pants at all. I wanted to be hot, wet and naked with his tongue—or his cock buried—deep.

"You're blushing, Vice Admiral." Kira was grinning at me like a besotted fool, which she was. Not that I could blame her. Warlord Anghar was an impressive warrior. And the truth was, no one could have forced me into the testing chair. I allowed Kira and Rachel to cajole me, to push me. The truth was I was tired of being alone.

"Fine." Tossing up my hands, I repeated, "Fine!"

All three of them exhaled and visibly relaxed, which only made me angrier with myself for showing weakness or doubt in the first place. "I'll transport."

The doctor stood and the next thing I knew, Kira and Rachel were pushing me out the door and toward the transport center, most likely before I changed my mind. I was on the transport pad and the doctor was working with the transport tech to arrange coordinates within minutes. I looked down at myself, ensuring my Coalition Fleet Vice-Admiral's uniform was in order and that I had my weapon strapped to my thigh. If I was leaving The Colony, I was taking everything with me.

Doctor Surnen cleared his throat and I looked at him, met his gaze. "It's tradition for females to arrive in more feminine clothing…"

I gave him an evil eye. "Don't push your luck, Doctor. I

want my potential mate to know exactly what he's dealing with."

The doctor actually grinned, which was a rare expression from a Prillon, especially on The Colony. "As you wish, my lady."

"I'm not a lady."

More grinning, but he kept his mouth shut. Definitely a smart Prillon.

"Give him hell, Niobe! Then make him beg for it." Kira laughed, her hands on her hips. The doctor turned to scowl at what he must have considered poor advice, but I ignored him and smiled back at her.

"I intend to." Beg. Push. Seduce. Chase me through a forest.

My pussy clenched again as the memories resurfaced. God, I couldn't wait.

"Don't do anything we wouldn't!" Rachel said from her position at the bottom of the steps to the raised platform.

"I'll give you three days, then I'm comm-ing you for details. *All* the details." Kira waggled her eyebrows and I glared.

"Deal." Hopefully, I would have some *details* to share. I turned my attention back to the doctor. "Where am I going, exactly? Everis?"

He glanced up quickly, then returned his gaze to the transport controls. "No, Vice Admiral. Elite Hunter Quinn is currently stationed with Battlegroup Karter in Sector 437. According to Coalition records, he is running Hive ReCon patrols from a subterranean base on Latiri 4."

The Karter? Sector 437? The doctor was sending me into the middle of a war zone. I knew it. Apparently, Kira did as well.

"Oh my God. That's the front line." Her gaze jumped from Doctor Surnen to me. "Maybe you *should* wait. He's not even on the battleship, Niobe. He's on the ground."

Elite Hunter Quinn.

Nice name. Quinn. My mind wandered momentarily. He was an Elite. He'd be strong. Fast. Maybe as fast as that warrior chasing me in my dreams…

"Niobe, no. You can't be serious. You should wait."

I was so preoccupied with imagining Quinn that it took me a moment to process what Kira said. "Wait. He's on the ground? I thought you said he was with Battleship Karter."

Doctor Surnen cleared his throat, looked at something on his tablet, then looked at me. "Normally, I would not be allowed to tell you this, nor would I be able to transport you to his location. But I see you have very high level I.C. clearance."

"I do." I knew just about everything going on in this war. Not all of it, but most. My work with the Intelligence Core was extensive and had been for years.

He sighed. "Elite Hunter Quinn is currently operating with a Hunter unit doing reconnaissance on the Hive. His unit is stationed in an underground facility behind enemy lines."

"What?" My mate was currently in Hive territory?

"The battle for Latiri 4 and Latiri 7 are pivotal in this war. Those two planets and their moons are perfectly positioned to operate as forward attack bases for several sectors of space. The Hive are not willing to give it up, and neither are we."

I knew that. I even knew we'd followed the Hive's lead and started building bases under the ground for the sole purpose of allowing them to overrun the territory. Once they were ensconced above the ground, unaware of our below-ground reconnaissance teams, we gathered significant amounts of intel on their movements, plans, and technological developments. I'd read about the new subterranean programs in an I.C. briefing several months ago. But reading about it and transporting to an underground fortress *beneath* Hive controlled territory were two very different things.

Kira and the doctor both looked at me. Did I want to wait?

No. Not really. But I wasn't stupid either.

"Is the base secure?"

The doctor checked his tablet again. "I'm sure you could check with better sources than me, but according to current data, yes."

I digested that one for a moment. "And how long is Quinn assigned to the base?"

His sigh was long and deep, and I knew I wasn't going to like the answer. "Indefinitely. Hunter units aren't like other Coalition assets. They cooperate with the Coalition Fleet, as long as it suits their agenda. He could leave tomorrow. He could be there for years. There are no firm orders. It is up to the Elite Hunter in charge of his unit, and their allegiances on Everis."

Yes, I could go back to the Academy and wait. Or, I could get on the transport pad and go on a wild adventure.

A tingle of excitement flooded my system. I hadn't been in combat in years, but the thought didn't frighten me. What made me want to shudder with dread was the idea of going back to my sparse office at the Academy and staring out that fucking window for one more day. Yes, what I did was important. I trained fighters. I made them smart. I saved lives. Occasionally, the I.C. would call me out for assignment. But these days, it was more diplomacy and spy games than open warfare. I was a desk-jockey, and it sucked the soul right out of me.

My primary job was to train new warriors, to make sure they could handle what they would find out there against the Hive. But I was bored. Lonely. A few days of excitement and hot sex sounded amazing.

"I spent over a decade in ReCon before I was promoted to serve at the Academy. I'm not afraid of getting dirty, Kira."

Kira was I.C., Intelligence Core. She and her mate, the Atlan warlord, still served. She knew me well enough to know I meant what I said. "I know." She didn't mention the I.C. aloud, as that was against protocol, but the look she gave me said she knew exactly what I was talking about. "It's not the dirt I'm worried about."

Rachel was laughing out loud when the vibrations of the transport pad traveled up from the soles of my feet. A second later, the hair on my arms stood on end.

"Your transport will occur in three... two... one."

Then my two friends were gone and I was once again on a transport pad.

Not on The Colony. On Latiri 4.

Instead of being welcomed by an Elite Hunter mate, I faced a Hive trio who looked as shocked as I felt. What the fuck was going on here?

All three raised their weapons in unison, three former Viken warriors covered in Hive technology. There was no light in their eyes. No soul. They were well and truly gone. Integrated.

Oh shit. Doctor Surnen needed to update his intel.

This was no Coalition controlled base.

This was Hive hell...

3

 uinn, Latiri 4, Hive Integration Base, Sector 437

THE TRANSPORT PAD VIBRATIONS MADE MY HEAD POUND where my cheek pressed to the cold, hard floor of my cell. No doubt even more prisoners were about to arrive on their way to hell, more warriors I couldn't save.

Fuck it all, I couldn't even save myself.

The last injection the Nexus bastard gave me was burning through my system like acid.

Worse, I could *hear* them now, inside my head, like the constant buzzing of insects on the trees back on Everis. Buzz. Rattle. Hum. The noise was constant. The headache made me grind my teeth in frustration. But I didn't stop fighting the noise, no matter how badly it hurt. If I gave in, they'd own me, and I'd rather be dead.

The trio of Hive who ran the transport pad moved

25

around like silent drones in perfect unison. Seeing Coalition warriors who'd been fully integrated and made into mindless machines was painful, but not as horrible as the idea of ending up exactly like them.

Empty.

Numb.

A weapon for the Nexus to wield against my fellow warriors.

This base was built to be a Coalition stronghold. Latiri 4 and Latiri 7, both in Sector 437 and under Commander Karter's protection, had been the front line of this war for a long time. Years. This sector of space was imperative for supply transport, and as a gateway for access to multiple inhabited planets.

The Coalition Fleet could not afford to lose control of this sector of space. So this underground base had been built in secret when this pile of rock was ours.

And then—we'd let them in. Let them take it. Let the Hive think they'd conquered ground and overrun our territory.

In truth, the whole thing had been a trap so we could gather intelligence from behind enemy lines. This base had been used to spy on Hive operations for almost a year now. The knowledge we'd acquired had begun to turn the odds in our favor.

Until about a week ago, when we'd been ambushed and overrun by Hive Soldiers and Drones. The Integration Units had moved in right behind them and the torture, deaths and *integrations* of my friends and fellow warriors had begun.

The Nexus had arrived on day two. His presence marked the end of the Elite Hunters under my command.

We'd been set aside. Special. The injections we'd received made the Hive's work on us invisible to the outside world.

But I could feel what they were doing to me. Inside. The microscopic technology moved through my cells like a virus, breaking things open. Repairing them. Changing me into something *else*.

I'd watched them turn this hidden sanctuary into a production facility for Hive Soldiers, wondering why no one came for us.

How was it possible that Battleship Karter didn't know what had happened here? We were required to report in to the Coalition with intel updates every few days. And I'd been in this cell for at least eight.

I blinked slowly as the transport pad's vibrations ceased. The trio of Viken drones froze as I watched, lifting their weapons in unison to face something I could not see.

Pushing up onto my hands and knees, I used the wall to pull myself upright, ignoring the pain slicing through the muscles in my legs. I knew from prior experience that once I was upright, the pain would fade.

"We did not authorize your transport, female. Where are your guards?" The leader of the trio spoke slowly and clearly, as if it were taking him a few minutes to process her presence. And had he just said *female*? What the fuck was a female doing here? There were female fighters, in great number, but they were sent elsewhere when captured. Or so I assumed, since I had not seen one come through the transport room for processing. Or out the same way, their minds gone, their bodies fully integrated and ready to fight those who'd been their friends and allies just days before.

Moving as close to the energy barrier as I could get, I froze. Listened. The force field would hold against an Atlan in full beast mode. I knew; I'd watched several pound themselves bloody trying to break free. I couldn't get past it, but I could be ready. Something felt off. Something felt... different, and it wasn't the buzzing in my skull. Anything that upset the Hive was good by me.

I waited for the unknown female to respond, as did the three Hive drones standing side by side in the transport room.

Instead of a response, ion blaster fire took all three out in rapid fire succession. Had she killed them? Was she a scout sent from Battleship Karter? The first strike of a ReCon team? Hope filled my head, making me dizzy.

Seconds later, a female in strange armor ran around to the back of the transport controls, her hands moving so quickly I had to focus to follow the movements. I blinked at the sight of her. She was gorgeous. Long, dark hair pulled back into a simple style I'd not seen before. Her armor covered every inch of her like a second skin, but it was the insignia on the armor that shocked me.

A vice admiral? Alone?

Was this supposed to be some kind of joke?

Who was this female? And why was she here?

"Hey! Over here!" I yelled at her and sighed in relief when her head lifted. She turned to face me and I stopped breathing, every cell in my body reacting to the female before me. Her dark brown gaze bored into mine like a gut punch and everything I'd suffered the last few days faded to nothing of import. The integrations, the torture, none of it mattered. What mattered was *her*. I needed to survive, not so I could fight another day, but so I could claim *her.* Bury my cock deep, master her body, make her scream my name. I'd never been one to believe in love at first sight, or the matching protocols. Not even the mark on my palm. I'd seen fellow Everians find their marked mate, saw the intense connection they shared, but never imagined it for myself.

My mark didn't burn, didn't awaken. She wasn't my marked mate. But that wasn't surprising. Less than one in a hundred, fewer, ever met a true marked mate. Most Everians chose their mates like those on many other worlds, attraction, respect, partnership.

Desire. The intangible connection between lovers. This female may not be my marked mate... but she would be mine.

I'd taken the bride test a long time ago. Every day I waited without an Interstellar Bride proved to me that I was right. The perfect female didn't exist. At least not for me.

Not until her. Fuck. *Her.*

I expected her to race to my cell and set me free. Instead, she tilted her head, probably hearing what I did— more Hive fighters running down the halls to reach her position. Was she Everian? Human? Viken? Definitely not Atlan. I couldn't tell from here, not without getting closer. Touching her. Smelling her skin. And the fucking energy barrier prevented it.

She turned back to the transport controls.

"Wait. They're coming!" I warned. I closed my eyes, counted footsteps. "Three more. Heavy." The footfalls were louder, the sound of movement lingered as if larger, slower bodies moved toward us. These would be either Prillon or Atlans who'd been integrated into Hive fighting machines. I knew the enemy liked to keep their most dangerous warriors around the perimeter, but the Atlan prisoners were also on this level, and it took one beast to battle another. The lighter, faster soldiers would be on the upper level, or guarding the flight decks. They weren't expecting an attack this deep inside the base. I hadn't either.

And was this an attack? One female hardly warranted much of a reaction. But then, she *had* just taken down three warriors before they could react.

The Hive had made a mistake in thinking they were safe here. Just as we had. And I'd make it far worse for them, if I ever got out of this cell.

The female ignored me, so I yelled again. "Over here! Shut down the energy field to my cell! I can help."

That got her attention. She leaned down and ripped an ion blaster from the hands of one of the dead Hive trio. An integrated Viken. Running over, she paused long enough to blast the control panel next to my cell. The energy field dropped instantly and I charged forward, taking the blaster from her hand.

"What is going on here? I thought this was a Coalition controlled base."

"It was, until just over a week ago. The Hive transported in and ran us over. We had no warning. Thought we were safe down here."

"Are there any more of you? Other prisoners?" she asked. But she wasn't looking at me. She was watching the hallway where I knew in about five seconds, three more Hive would appear. Bigger this time. Stronger.

"Many have been transported in. I've seen every one of them. How many are left alive, I have no fucking idea."

I listened again. If I had to guess, I'd say one Atlan and two Prillon warriors. Shit. They wouldn't go down from a single hit from a blaster. No, they would be much harder to kill.

Something in my tone caught her attention because that dark gaze returned to me, either sadness or pity in her eyes. I couldn't decide which and wanted neither.

"Take cover. I'll take them out." I didn't need a pity party. Now that I was free, with a weapon in my hand, the buzzing helpless feeling in my head could go fuck itself.

"Three of them are going to be on us in a few seconds. And one of them is… was an Atlan."

"I know."

She knew? How? She could hear them, too?

She wasn't looking at me, not anymore. She'd done as I suggested and had taken cover behind the corner, only her shoulder and her ion blaster a target for the Hive.

Her gaze narrowed and her aim was steady.

Gods help me, she was magnificent. How the hell had she heard the distinct difference in the heavy footfalls of the integrated Atlan? I'd known, but I had Hunter's senses. She was not an Elite Hunter. I didn't know what she was, other than beautiful—I glanced at the three dead Viken Hive on the floor behind her—and lethal. Efficient. Ruthless.

"Who are you?" I couldn't help but ask, even as we awaited the enemy. She was a mystery. A complete and total mystery I very much wanted to solve. "And how did you get here?"

Transport, obviously. But how had she gotten the coordinates? How had she known about this secret Hive integration center?

Of course, the vexing female ignored the questions.

She glanced up at me, her dark eyes sharp. "Are you going to stand there like a target, or are you going to help me get us out of here?"

I recognized the language as one common to Earth. Was she human? And if so, how had she heard the integrated soldiers coming? Or believed one to be an Atlan? Humans were known for their tenacity and courage, not for their superior senses.

"Take cover, warrior. Now."

That tone of voice—of a commander used to being obeyed—was one I'd not heard from a female often, and definitely not from any female as petite and beautiful as she. I didn't care what planet she was from. Here, in the middle of a fucking integration center, I got hard. My cock didn't seem to care that we were about to be set upon by the enemy. It wanted her. And her dominance. Oh, it did something for me. Made my inner Hunter want to show her who was really in charge. Maybe not in this moment, but once I got that uniform off that delectable body, she'd know it was me.

I grinned. Oh yes. I was the Hunter and she was going to quickly discover she was the hunted.

A roar echoed down the corridor, the integrated Atlan in beast mode, gave us warning. With the Atlans, I never knew if they were completely gone to the Hive implants, or still fighting. Sometimes, they would delay a killing blow to give a ReCon team or warrior on the battlefield time to take them down.

A quick death was a mercy.

Positioning myself to cover the female's position, I checked the power level on the weapon. It was fully charged, and I set the ion pistol to maximum damage. "I'll hold them off. Do you know how to work transport controls?"

She glanced back at me, over her shoulder, the look full of irritation, her lips tight and thin. "Keep them off us and I'll get us out of here. We'll have to come back for any other prisoners."

"Done."

She stood, turning so her back was to the wall as I continued to cover the corridor. "What's your name?" she asked.

"Quinn."

She blinked slowly, as if my name startled her and her gaze roamed my face with intense interest. With something more than simple fighting instinct. "You're Everian? An Elite Hunter?"

I nodded. "I am." She seemed to know a lot about my kind. Unusual. Most of the aliens I'd met from Earth barely knew my planet existed.

"Good. Then you should be able to keep them off me."

It was my turn to be irritated. "Of course."

She grinned, the mischief in her eyes made me want to kiss her. Fuck. Who was I kidding, I wanted to slam her against the wall and bury my cock deep. But that would have to wait until we got off this rock. I'd silence that sass. Turn it into gasps. Breathy moans of pleasure.

Without another word, she dashed to the control panel, and I turned back to the hallway as the first attacker appeared. The integrated Atlan beast was front and center. The ceilings on this base were ten feet tall, and still he ducked as if afraid he'd strike the top of his head.

He wouldn't, unless he leaped for a kill.

I fired, non-stop, until the beast hit his knees. Like water flowing around a rock, the other two moved in front of him and kept coming. Prillon warriors, or at least they used to be. They were not my main concern. Two shots for each and they were down, writhing on the ground as the Atlan behind them fought to stand.

"Hurry," I called. "The beast is coming again."

"I'm working on it." The female was bent over the control panel, her fingers flying furiously. The concentration on her face was another fascinating addition to her repertoire, but I didn't have time to stare, as I would have preferred. I filed the image away for later when I would be able to take my time, perhaps trace her lips with my fingertips as I watched her expression change under my touch.

"We. Kill." The integrated Atlan was in full beast mode, and apparently, he—they—the trio of Hive, had received orders to kill me. Most likely, they would kill *her* as well.

"Not today." I fired, taking my time, hitting the vulnerable spots in the beast's armor. His neck. His knees. His face, when I could take time for an extra shot.

I heard his helmet crack and fought down a shout of victory. As I watched, he took his helmet off and threw it aside, forgotten.

Gods, he was fucking huge.

I didn't want to kill him. I didn't. One head shot would take him down now, but I knew him. Had worked with him for the last few months. Before being captured. Since the Hive invasion of this base, I hadn't seen him once. Until now. Until he'd been integrated enough to be under their control. To fight, to try to kill me.

He was a good male. Honorable. A true warrior.

"Damn you, Zan."

Adjusting the settings on my blaster, I hoped the lower setting would knock him unconscious, not kill him. The Prillon warriors I'd killed were not from this base. They were not newly integrated, as this Atlan was. They were old converts, their minds long gone, only shells now, bodies with so many integrations they were all Hive. All enemy. I'd heard that the Hive would pair conquered, reliable soldiers like these two Prillons with the Atlans in a bid to help control their beasts.

With the integrated Prillon warriors down, there was no hope of that. Zan was charging me now, completely out of his mind.

Fuck.

I raised my rifle, took aim. Fired a stun shot.

His head snapped back and he toppled like a felled tree. Racing forward, I checked him for a pulse.

Still breathing. Good. The stun setting had worked, even on a beast.

Pausing to listen, I heard the female cursing under her breath as more footsteps headed our way. Clearly, she could hear them as well. They were probably two corridors back, but we only had a few minutes. Three at the most. And there were more than three this time. A *lot* more.

And the Atlan was huge but he needed saving. I couldn't leave him here if there was a chance of him surviving, even if it was on The Colony.

I grabbed the only thing I could manage to wrap one arm around and pulled him by the leg into the transport room. The three transport techs she'd killed were on the floor, dead. Ignored. The female looked up from the control panel, glanced at the Atlan, and frowned.

"He's a friend." Zan was an honorable warrior, I would not leave him behind. And none of us would be leaving if that blue bastard made his way down here. "Get us out of here before the Nexus unit arrives. Zan won't stand a chance against him if he wakes up."

Her movement stalled. "There is a Nexus unit on this base?"

"Yes." I wasn't sure how or why she knew what a Nexus was, as the information was for top level operatives and commanders only, but I was too busy wrangling the beast's oversized body into position to ask.

"We've got bigger problems. Incoming transport and I can't override the command. It's too late."

I dropped Zan's leg, leaving him stunned and sprawled on the floor. There wasn't much space to maneuver with him taking up most of the space along with the dead transport techs. I turned to face the transport pad. As she'd warned, the buzzing charge filled the air and vibrations moved through my feet. "Friendly?"

"No. I don't think so." She grabbed the weapons from the dead techs, tossed me one. I checked the settings, armed it. Never hurt to have two weapons instead of one. "They're bringing more Coalition fighters... prisoners, to integrate."

Readying her own ion pistol and taking a knee, she now had a weapon armed and ready in each hand, like me. She used the control panel as cover. Waited.

"How many?" I asked.

"Seven."

Fuck. That was a lot, if they were all Hive. "The Hive

work in threes. Always. They're fucking consistent. There wouldn't be two groups for one prisoner. It'll be three guards with four prisoners. Happens several times a day. I know." Unfortunately, I knew all too well.

She nodded but didn't look my way. I returned my attention to the pad as seven figures appeared.

It was easy to distinguish Hive from Coalition. Easy to aim. Fire. Kill. The three Hive guards, just as I'd expected, hadn't imagined being ambushed within their own facility. Prisoners didn't escape. Didn't fight back.

But I did. So did... she. She took down two of them nearly as quickly as I did one. She was magnificent. Fuck, I didn't even know her name.

The four Coalition fighters dropped to their knees and lowered their heads in protection. They could do nothing else they'd been trained to do. They had no weapons. They were restrained.

It was over in seconds. The guards dead. The prisoners looked up, took in where they were, what had happened.

"Where the fuck are we?" A Prillon asked, probably noticing it was a Coalition transport pad he'd arrived on.

"Latiri 4. I'll explain more later. Get the Atlan onto the pad. We're getting out of here," she ordered.

She was already ignoring me, expecting me to do as I was told as her fingers flew over the controls. Damn the woman, I wanted her, and I wanted to bend her to my will, conquer her body and soul. This wasn't the time or place to argue, however. And, she was right.

I took an electronic key from the nearest dead integrated Viken's hip and motioned for the four prisoners to come to me. They did, without delay, and I released their bonds. The nearest, a fierce looking Prillon warrior the others seemed to defer to, motioned the other three toward the Atlan.

"You have your orders, get this Atlan onto the transport pad."

The female behind the controls glanced up at the sound of his voice. "Good to see you, Prax. It's been a long time."

The Prillon captain, Prax, grinned at her. She grinned back, the expression a new one, and not directed at me. I blinked, trying not to stare. Gods, she was fucking gorgeous. And who was she that this Prillon knew who she was *and* followed her orders without question? The Prillon wore a captain's markings on his uniform, and I didn't doubt his assessment of the situation. The two obviously knew one another, but how?

And did she belong to him? Was she his mate? Had he made a claim on my female?

My female. The thought raced through my head even as I handed the unknown Prillon captain my spare blaster and helped tug the giant Atlan onto the transport pad.

We worked as a team to hoist him up to the platform. Even five strong fighters struggled with the beast. Once we had him where he'd be transported with us, I handed off my weapon to another of the fighters and moved to the female's side. I took her spare as well, tossed it to a third warrior and lifted the small ion pistol from where she had placed it within reach on top of the control panel.

The warriors settled into a defensive position around the unconscious Atlan and I moved between my female and the open door. I could hear the Hive coming, knew the prisoners would fight to the death, more than happy to shoot any Hive who fucked with us now.

"Can you get us out of here?" I asked her. She had been at the controls for what felt like hours, working those small hands with quick, deft movements.

"Yes. But I'm locking down the entire base first."

What did she just say?

I turned to face her. "How?"

She didn't even look at me, speaking instead to the control panel. "Initiate Lockdown Protocol. Command Code…" She rattled off a few words in the home language of Prillon Prime and waited. Something beeped and her shoulders sagged in relief. "They didn't get into the main system. My command codes still work."

What just happened? No one could lock down an entire base. It wasn't conceivable. "That's impossible."

"I have Level Two command codes, Hunter. No one will get in or out of this base without my permission. Not anymore." She glanced at me as she moved away from the control panel, toward the Prillon captain. I retreated from the door, moving closer as much because I didn't like her being so close to the warrior as because it was time to transport out of this hell.

Level Two command codes?

Level One was Prime Nial himself, leader of the entire Coalition Fleet, ruler of the Coalition of Planets. He controlled everything. If what she said was true, only the Prime himself could override her lockdown of this base.

Battleship commanders, like Commander Karter, only had Level Four codes. Mine were Level Five.

Fuck. Exactly who was she?

"Let's go." Captain Prax shifted on his feet. "I need to check on the rest of my men."

I didn't have the heart to tell him they were probably

already locked down in cells deeper inside the base, being integrated. Destroyed.

The female jumped onto the transport pad and the Prillon captain positioned himself between her and the corridor in a protective stance, not just that of a warrior protecting a helpless female. There was too much knowledge in his eyes. Respect.

Who *was* she? I.C.? I didn't know any fighters with command codes. Unless she was just the victim of an accident and a transport tech had accidentally sent her to the wrong place.

Yeah, no. She was too intelligent, too quick and keen for something as ridiculous as that. And if something that random had brought her to me, that transport tech was most likely headed for a Coalition brig.

I felt the vibrations, heard the hum.

"Everyone ready?" she asked, glancing up at the six of us on the transport pad. It had been about a minute since the prisoners arrived, and they were being sent right back out of here. They were lucky.

So fucking lucky. The Atlan who was dead weight at their feet, too.

"Fuck, yes," I said. The others shouted and growled their agreement. They'd been defeated, but their fight was back. We were getting the fuck out of here.

I heard the pounding of feet with my Hunter senses. "Incoming," I said.

She nodded, either she believed me or could hear them, too. It wasn't time to wonder which.

"Five seconds," she said.

I moved with speed to stand beside her. I tipped up her

chin so she'd look at me. Made her take one of those five seconds to focus on me.

"Who are you?" I asked. The hairs on my body stood on end from the impending transport.

Three seconds.

Two seconds. The team of Hive ran into the room. Out of the corner of my eye, I saw their weapons raised. The other warriors fired at them, but I ignored it all. I could only see her. See the female who'd saved my life. The lives of six warriors.

"I'm your mate."

One second.

And we were gone. Transporting out of the Hive hell and to safety. With my...

Mate.

4

*N*iobe, *Battleship Karter, Sector 437*

I REALLY HADN'T MEANT TO SPRING IT ON HIM LIKE THAT.

I'm your mate.

Not exactly me at my most brilliant. I hadn't even told him my name.

But then again, I *had* transported into the middle of a Hive Integration base—an *unknown* Integration Base that was supposed to be one of ours—and been forced to fight for my life, and his, as soon as I'd had time to blink. Good thing I didn't travel without my weapon. Good thing my instincts and reflexes hadn't gotten rusty running the Academy. My I.C. commander would laugh at the very thought.

All in all, my years on a battleship ReCon team had paid off in a big way. The old training had kicked back in instantly, like I'd never been gone, let alone spent the last few years sitting behind a desk, or training new Coalition cadets.

I wasn't surprised by the shocked expression of the transport officer on Commander Karter's ship when seven fighters transported without prior approval or planning. I *had* input an override protocol that placed us deep inside the nearest battleship, as far from the Hive as I could get us in the shortest amount of time.

I could have transported us anywhere. The Academy. Everis. Prillon Prime. None of those made sense considering where we'd been. What we knew.

The Karter was the perfect choice. Not only was it in the same sector as the hidden Hive base, but it was the only battleship close enough to mount an assault on the Hive there. They were using *our* base to torture and kill *our* warriors, right under our noses, and the faster we took care of the problem, the more warriors we could save.

The fact that the Coalition hadn't known the base had been overrun by the enemy enraged me. I knew Commander Karter, the tough as nails Prillon Commander. I'd worked with him on numerous I.C. missions with Commander Chloe Phan. I was confident Commander Karter would act quickly, would show no mercy.

I'd locked that secret base down and trapped any remaining Hive like rats in a barrel. The transport codes would prevent any movement in or out, unless I personally authorized the transport—or Prime Nial himself chose to override my codes. No. Nothing was getting into or out of that base until we had enough warriors to go in there and clean house, save our people, and take care of this mess.

Quinn hadn't known how many others were still down there, alive and trapped with the Hive. How could he know an exact count when he'd been in a cell behind an energy barrier and the Hive were a bunch of ruthless assholes? We had to go back. I wouldn't risk any fighter's life to that hellhole. He wouldn't either, considering what the Hive had probably put him through. Who knew what integrations he had, or what tortures he'd survived.

The warrior behind the transport control panel looked up at us, his jaw gaping for a moment before he regained control of himself. The vibrations ceased, my hair stopped crackling. "Who are you?" he asked. Stunned. Definitely confused. "You are not on my transport list." He glanced at the Prillon captain behind me, a cadet I'd trained several years ago. A good warrior and an honorable male. "Captain Prax? Is that you? You were reported missing on Latiri 7. How did you end up here?"

Prax growled as the Atlan at our feet began to stir, his ion blaster pointed at the warrior who'd resumed his normal form, which was still about three hundred pounds and a solid seven feet. The beast was gone now. We didn't know the extent of his integrations. Hell, we didn't even know if he could be saved.

I stepped off the pad, down the platform's steps. "I'm Vice Admiral Niobe. I need to see Commander Karter and Commander Phan immediately."

The male's hand moved swiftly to verify my identity, as was protocol. I waited impatiently, my booted foot tapping on the floor of the transport room as the screen behind him mirrored what he was seeing on the control panel. An image of my face appeared, along with my service record and a large emblem in the upper corner confirming I was a vice admiral—not that he could miss that rank by looking at my uniform—and my status as a member of the I.C. The male glanced at me, then down, then back up. "At once, Vice Admiral. I will inform the commanders of your arrival."

"Good." I nodded, trying to ignore the Hunter behind me, my *mate,* who was moving in close. Too close, like an alpha male. A very protective one. I shifted a few steps away because I needed to stay in control. Breathing in his scent, feeling the heat coming from his body, the look in his gaze... it was distracting. And nipple hardening.

"Alert medical." I tipped my head toward the platform. "I have an integrated Atlan here, and four rescued prisoners from a Hive Integration facility. They were new arrivals there and have no new integrations that I am aware of, but they need a thorough medical exam just in case."

The tech nodded. "Yes, Vice Admiral."

He stood, staring at all of us for another few seconds, taking in the battle worn prisoners, the Everian Hunter, the unconscious Atlan full of Hive tech, and me.

I raised my eyebrows. I didn't have time for this kind of nonsense. "Now."

He jumped as if stung by a bee and a few seconds later a medical team in green raced into the transport room. The Atlan was injected with what I assumed was a strong sedative as the others were led out of the room to the medical station. Captain Prax nodded his head, either in thanks or goodbye or any other possibility. I was just glad he was safe. Whole.

I lifted a hand, signaled one doctor to remain. He nodded slightly and waited for my orders. There was one very stubborn Everian I knew who needed to be tended. I also knew he wasn't going to allow it, not until he'd spoken to me. To tell him I was his mate then transport to a battleship? Yeah, probably not the way it was usually done.

I turned on my heel. I knew Quinn hadn't gone with the others. I felt him watching me, devouring me with his gaze. Intense. Sensual. Needy.

"How long were you a prisoner?" I asked. I didn't want to know, and I did. My heart, which hadn't even known he existed just a short time ago, ached for him now. While I'd been on The Colony with Kira and Angh and the others there, he'd been tortured.

"I lost count of the days. A week. Maybe longer."

I could only imagine. The base was underground. No windows. No light. No space to use to get one's bearings. He stepped closer, lifted a hand to my face, traced my cheek with his fingertips. For a Hunter, and I knew he was an Elite, his touch was gentle, the motion slow.

"Is what you said true? Are you mine?" he asked, his voice soft.

"Yes." There was no reason to deny our match. "And you are mine." I wanted to get that out there from the beginning. I was not a soft, submissive female. I would demand as much as I gave. Perhaps more.

"By the gods." He leaned in close, nuzzled the side of my neck as I motioned the doctor in closer. "What is your name?"

"Niobe."

He repeated the name, breathed me in. His hands came to rest on my hips and I swayed, the adrenaline from battle and his nearness combining to overwhelm me for a few seconds. But no more. He'd been tortured. Integrated. He was hurt. Too thin. The circles under his eyes spoke of long days without sleep. The lines around his mouth reflections of pain. And I could only imagine the mental hardships he'd endured. "You need to go to medical, Quinn."

"I'm fine. I'll be fine. I need you, not a doctor."

I laughed, I couldn't help myself, the sound a surprise even to me. He was feisty, my mate. "I was afraid you were going to say that."

That got his attention and he lifted his head to stare into my eyes. "Niobe."

"Quinn."

"I want to kiss you."

God yes. *Kiss me.* I nodded at the doctor behind him. "Alright. And then you go to medical."

"Then I make you mine," he growled.

Before I could reply to that, his lips crushed mine, stealing my breath, my sanity. His touch made my body burn, and I had to use every ounce of discipline I had to raise a hand from his back and signal the doctor to get in close, inject him, knock him out.

I knew the moment it was done, for Quinn sagged against me, our lips still touching. As his knees buckled, his eyes opened and he held my gaze. A hand covered the injection spot on his neck. "You're going to get a spanking for this."

I laughed again. God help me, he was charming. And that was fucking hot. No one had spanked me—not as a

47

child for punishment—or as an adult for play. Ever. But the idea of Quinn doing it? My panties were ruined.

First, he needed a thorough medical exam, some time in a ReGen pod. He needed to heal, and if he were like any other male alien in the universe when discovering he had a mate, he wasn't going to be distracted. He was mine, and I was going to take care of him whether he wanted me to or not. Whether I got a spanking for it or not.

I smiled as the doctor caught him from behind and the transport officer came around to help carry my mate to the medical station. He grinned at me, awake but sedated, his body collapsing before his mind. He stared, and those amber eyes were filled with a dark vow.

I couldn't help myself, couldn't stop the naughty side of me from taunting him.

"Promises, promises, mate."

He kept smiling as they carried him away. I was grinning like an idiot, replaying the entire scene in my mind, when Commander Karter entered the transport room.

"Vice Admiral." His voice boomed. "What the fuck is going on? And how did you get on my battleship?"

———

Two hours later

Quinn – Medical Unit

EVEN BEFORE I OPENED MY EYES, I KNEW WHERE I WAS, THE

all too familiar scent of the interior of a ReGen pod filling my head with dozens of memories I had no desire to relive. Still, it was better than that underground prison I'd been trapped in. I was naked, but the stench of the Nexus and his torments were gone. I had no doubt the doctor had examined every molecule in my body, searching for Hive technology, trying to assess the danger I might present to the crew.

And I was different. The buzzing in my mind was gone, but my body felt hyper-aware, every pressure point on the healing bed acutely present in my senses. The scent of the cleansing solution used on Coalition ships. The feminine allure of my mate somewhere close.

This was far from the first time I'd awakened inside a ReGen pod, but this time was unique. This time *she* was here. I felt her, heard her heartbeat, her voice as she and Commander Karter spoke intensely on the other side of the pod.

The fact that she'd remained by my side made my heart race. My mate was no ordinary female. She was a vice admiral in the Coalition Fleet and far outranked me. Based on her movements and her speech, I assumed she was human, from Earth... and yet that did not feel quite right.

Her scent reminded me of home, of Everis, and I wondered if she was from my world instead. Perhaps she had spent time hunting on Earth and picked up their customs and language. Everian Hunters were masters at blending in, mimicking accents, mannerisms, the multitude of indescribable details that made one stand out as *other*.

If she were Everian, and not human, then I wondered

which Elite Hunter had sired her. Was her father a legend on my home world, or an unknown?

Not that I cared about her history. I couldn't care less where she had been in the past, as long as she was with me now. But I was a predator with an insatiable curiosity, a curiosity that she stirred more strongly than anything ever had before. I wanted to know everything about her. Every. Single. Detail. From birth to this moment.

She was mine.

The clear lid lifted automatically and both my mate and Commander Karter came over. I sat up, wiped a hand over my face.

"How do you feel?" the commander asked.

My mate's gaze raked over my body. Every bare inch. And, of course, that made me hard.

"Get this man a sheet," the commander shouted, waving his arm. He'd seen that my cock hadn't been injured and probably wasn't thrilled to have a conversation with me with it right out there.

I couldn't help it. My mate was before me. Unclaimed.

The doctor came over and handed me a white sheet, and I laid it over my lap.

"As you saw, I'm fine." I looked to the doctor. "What about integrations?"

He looked to the tablet he held. "The data shows a multitude of microscopic integrations. There is only one other warrior on record with this type of integration, a Prillon male on The Colony. His name is Tyran. I have reviewed his file, and the type of implant you and he received does not appear to affect your mind until complete saturation level is achieved. Your cellular saturation is at eighty-five percent."

Fuck. One or two more injections from that blue fucker and he would have had me.

The doctor was still talking. "The integrations will make your muscles much stronger and more resilient than before. Your bones as well. I believe the Prillon, Tyran, has been tested and is stronger than the integrated Atlans on Base 3. As long as you do not receive any additional integration treatments, you'll be fine. Stronger. Faster. But fine. As to your general health. You were sleep deprived, malnourished and dehydrated, but the ReGen pod did its job."

"Thank you." He spoke true. My body hummed with vitality. Life.

Need.

I looked to my mate, unchanged from when I'd seen her earlier. But we were no longer in a fight for our lives with the Hive. We were safe on the battleship. I was healed. Nothing but a commander stood in the way of me making her mine.

That and a fucking shower tube.

"I need to bathe. Commander, if I may…"

"Not yet. How many days have the Hive controlled our base?" The commander's gaze was dark, unrelenting. I recognized fury when I saw it, and the Prillon commander was vibrating with rage, every muscle taut, shaking with a barely controlled need to attack.

"At least a week. I counted eight days in my cell, but I could have been off in either direction. There was no clock or changes in lighting. I had to guess based on their shift changes."

He paced in front of me, every few steps blocking my view of Niobe, but she was no longer focused on me. Her frown was nearly as severe as the commander's. "Commander Karter, how is it that you had a Coalition base captured by the Hive more than a week ago, and you had no idea the attack had happened?"

He growled and whirled to face her, but his voice was respectful, even if filled with anger. "Vice Admiral, we received reports, at the scheduled intervals, from the base. They had the correct passcodes and relayed expected information. We had no way of knowing. They mimicked our procedures perfectly."

Her gaze drifted to me, the heat returning, if tempered by our circumstances. "Am I to infer that this could be occurring at other Coalition bases and we would have no indication that anything was wrong?"

He stepped back. Nodded. "Yes."

My gorgeous mate cursed and stepped away, moving toward the door for some illusion of privacy. "I need to report this. It had to be the presence of the Nexus unit."

Commander Karter froze. "What did you just say?" He turned to look at me. "Is there a Nexus trapped on that base?"

"Yes." When I confirmed the news, Commander Karter's tension slipped into something cold and measured. Calculating. "Take your shower, Quinn. Spend time with your mate. You have two hours, and not a moment longer. Do you understand me? If you two are one minute late to the the command deck for the debriefing, vice admiral or not, I will personally pound down your door."

The idea made me chuckle, until I looked up into the face of a seriously enraged Prillon warrior. He was ready to tear things to pieces, to rend and pound and kill. Tick-tock. If he didn't need time to assemble the assault teams, we'd probably be heading for the transport rooms in attack formation now. "I understand. Those are my men down there, too. He already killed my entire Hunter unit. No one wants him dead more than I do."

Commander Karter tilted his head, as if listening to Niobe's conversation with someone. She said she had to make a call. Report. But to whom?

The doctor pointed. "A shower tube is there."

I climbed from the unit, stood before my mate with just my hand holding the sheet over my hard cock as she ended her communication. I had no idea who she was talking to, and I didn't care. I tucked her hair back from her face as I took in every inch of her features. Dark eyes. Freckles on her pert nose. Full lips, but in a severe line. She looked tense. Worried. Oh, that would change as soon as I fucked her. "Soon, mate."

"Elite Hunter, get your ass in that shower tube," Karter commanded. "And cover it on your way there."

After so many days of suffering, of pain, this unexpected turn of events was akin to being reborn. I had survived. I had a gorgeous mate, and vengeance would be mine in a matter of hours. The warmth I felt when I looked at Niobe was a spark of joy I desperately needed. I winked at my mate, then walked over to the shower tube, ignoring the commander. I could hear my mate's intake of breath, could smell her arousal.

"Doctor, get a tech to S-Gen that fighter a uniform. Stat."

Stepping under the hot water, I sighed. Laughed. Fuck, it felt good to be free. To know my mate awaited me.

Five minutes later, I was dressed in a full Elite Hunter

uniform, a newly generated one that no longer smelled like misery. Karter stood just where he'd been, arms crossed over his chest. I saw that out of the corner of my eye, for I wasn't looking at him. I was looking at my mate. *Niobe.*

"Two hours," he said.

I didn't look his way. She wasn't a small female. Long-limbed, her body was lush and full. Toned and well-muscled, even beneath the uniform's armor. I wanted to peel off every bit of clothing and learn her, inch by inch.

"Elite Hunter," the commander said.

"Yes?" I asked, taking in the full swells of Niobe's breasts, the way they raised and fell with her every breath. She *was* aroused. I could scent it. Her cheeks flushed and that was the only outward sign she offered that she was anything but the serious vice admiral she let everyone see. The pink in her cheeks let me know that she'd been caught. She was just as eager for me as I was for her.

"Elite Hunter," Karter repeated.

"Yes?" I asked him again.

"I'm over here." He sighed. "If I had not learned from the vice admiral that you were recently matched, I would throw you in the brig for insubordination."

"Thank you."

"I don't want your appreciation; I want your attention."

I met Niobe's dark gaze. Held it. Mesmerized. "With all due respect, Commander, I can't give you my attention right now."

He sighed again. "Yes, I can see that. You have two hours off-duty and then I expect to see you both on the command deck."

"How long will Zan be in his ReGen Pod?" I asked. He'd been all over the Hive-controlled base where I'd only made it as far as the cell by the transport room. He knew what was going on there better than me. Better than anyone alive.

"Zan?"

"The Atlan we brought in."

"Six more hours," the doctor told us.

"Then I have six hours with my mate. Zan was fully integrated. While I was locked in a cell, he was everywhere. He'll know how many guards they have, where they are stationed, how many prisoners remain. We need him healed. We need his intel on that base. First, Zan heals. Then we debrief and get back down there. Save everyone who's left."

Niobe frowned. Yeah, she didn't like leaving fellow fighters in a hell like that either.

"Fine. Six hours," Karter repeated. "While you two are... getting to know each other, I'll get a ReCon team to examine the plans we have for that base, get the assault teams ready."

When neither of us looked his way, the commander grumbled to himself, something about mates and insanity.

"Six hours, Vice Admiral." Now he was speaking to my mate, perhaps hoping he'd get more of her attention. Not happening. "I remember being in your place. Erica would kill me if I didn't give you two time."

But he'd only give it to us now since we had to wait for Zan to recover. I understood. Claiming my mate would wait until the search and rescue was over under any other circumstances, but the gods were being kind today... and I would taste her.

We had six hours. Six. Hours.

He stalked off, left us. We were alone in the ReGen room—besides Zan, who was healing in one of the pods—but I didn't care if there was an entire battalion of fighters behind us.

I had Niobe in front of me. I could do nothing while the commander readied his teams. Nothing but fuck and get to know the female of my heart. It was time to *have* her.

5

"I HAVE BEEN WAITING FOR YOU," QUINN SAID. THE admission was revealing, exposing the inner core of an Elite Hunter which I had no doubt was never shown. Only with...

A mate.

We barely knew each other. We'd met just a few hours ago. Hours. A lot had happened to me today. I'd been on The Colony and been tested, bickered with Kira and Rachel. Then transported to a secret Hive integration center and rescued not only my matched mate, but other fighters as well. Another transport had us on the Karter where I'd stared at my mate inside a ReGen pod while speaking to Commander Karter and planning an attack on the base I'd just left behind.

I should be weary from a battle, double transport, the

adrenaline dump, meeting a *mate...* but I wasn't. Far from it. I felt alive and invigorated in a way I'd never imagined. Was it this male's amber colored eyes boring into me? Was it the way his muscles shifted and played beneath the lines of his fresh uniform? Was it the connection, the invisible threads that connected us, no matter how much I fought the instinct to snip them and bolt?

I wasn't baring my soul to him. I didn't do that with people I'd known for years, let alone a few hours. It didn't matter that he was my testing match, that I *should* share everything with him. My body, my heart, my soul. I didn't know him. Not yet. But I wanted to. Longed for a deeper connection, for someone who was mine.

"I was waiting for you. You were the one in a ReGen pod, unconscious."

"Before that, mate. I've been waiting a lot longer than that," he replied. It wasn't the words that made stupid leap out of my mouth, it was the look in his eyes. Possessive. Hungry. Impatient. A look that made my legs tingle and my nipples go hard. The look in his eyes was a challenge, and the Everian in me was rising to meet it. To *run*. Just like in my matching dream, I wanted to force him to prove himself worthy. Fast. Strong enough to catch me.

To conquer me.

Shit. Where had *that* thought come from?

"You had no idea I would arrive at that prison." I said the last few words as if they were poison. That place... god, it had been awful. I didn't want to think about what would have happened to him or the others if I hadn't ended up there. At that exact moment. How long would he have survived if I hadn't taken the Interstellar Brides' Program test?

"I wasn't referring to your timely transport and you know it," he replied. He was so calm, so… even. I breathed in his clean scent, even underneath the medical unit's strong soap.

Hunters resolved problems with a demeanor of ease, of confidence. They didn't go beast like the Atlans or have a second like the Prillons. We were independent. Smooth. Deadly.

With Quinn, I was far from smooth. I felt… frazzled now that he was whole. Wary. Off kilter. Uncomfortable because I was out of my element. No, that wasn't it.

It was six hours. We had six hours to play. To make love. To get to know one another.

And even though my body was screaming "yes-yes-yes!" my mind didn't like giving up control. And I felt guilt creeping in, guilt that I was alive and whole and full of desire for my mate when there was an unknown number of warriors suffering on that base. Waiting. For me.

For us.

It seemed Quinn could shift his focus easier than me. My mate was looking at me as if I were his dinner. And *that* had my body responding. Panicking. I had no control. A mission? Yes. A mate? Hell, no. I was grasping, trying to cling to the last shreds of calm that I could find, and that completely messed with my mind.

"Mate, your need is nothing to fear, it is a need we share." His deep voice was even, almost soothing.

"We don't share anything." I held up my hand so he could see my palm, the mark there. "We're not marked mates. Just matched."

Even as I said the words, I didn't believe them. We

shared quite a bit, I just didn't understand it, and it was a bit scary.

He shrugged those big, brawny shoulders and it made my nipples go hard. Traitors. I crossed my arms over my chest.

The corner of his mouth tipped up. He breathed deep, nostrils flaring. "You are mine. You know it. I know it. *Everyone* on this ship knows it. Why are you resisting?"

Why was I? Oh yeah, I didn't need a bossy male. My pussy was arguing with me about that, but I was in control... at least of my body.

Except my nipples ached and lower, I was wet for him. And he knew it. Could smell it. That rough tumble of a voice wasn't helping me fight my libido at all.

"I can't give you what you want," I told him. I didn't have to bare my soul, but I had my reasons. This was a mistake. It had to be. I didn't want kids. I didn't want to give up my life, my freedom, my career. I made a difference in this war. I trained cadets, made sure they were ready for the Hive. I tried to save lives, and my work was important to me, too important. I never should have given in to a moment of weakness, of loneliness. Elite Hunter Quinn of Everis probably wanted a submissive little wife and ten babies running around the house chasing each other and screaming up a storm.

That life wasn't for me. I wasn't meant to be with someone. Shit. I screwed this up. "I never should have taken the bride testing."

His pale gaze raked over me some more, from the top of my head to the boots on my feet. Leisurely, as if he had all the time in the world. As if he had every right to do so.

"I disagree. You are perfect and I can't wait to bury my cock in your body, make you come. Make you mine.

Oh fuck. I may have just come a little bit. "You don't know me."

"This is true, mate, but I will." His words weren't a threat, they were a vow, a promise. He was a Hunter and I was beginning to fully understand what it meant to have the full attention of an Elite male from Everis. He would never stop. Never give in.

The thoughts spun in my mind like a tornado. This couldn't be real, could it? Was he really mine?

No. No way. He didn't even know me yet. I had thirty days to reject the match and go back to my old, predictable, responsible life. Thirty days, too, for him to decide he wanted fifteen babies and someone ten years younger.

Whatever. This was bullshit. Mental, emotional, physical bullshit. I never should have let Kira talk me into this. I should have said no, gone home and opened a bottle of Atlan wine. A vibrator didn't want children or demand submission. Demand secrets. Truth. Trust.

What *had* I been thinking?

Spinning on my heel, I strode for the door. It slid open silently and I walked out. Didn't stop once I exited the medical unit.

He didn't follow. Over all the sounds of the battleship, from the low vibration of the engines to the clinking of dishes in the cafeteria on the floor below, I could hear Quinn. His breathing, the slow beat of his heart. He hadn't moved.

Down the hall, I pushed the button for the lift not knowing where I was going. I just needed to get away, to get control again. The closer I was to him, the less I had of it. Damn him!

"You can run, mate, but I *will* catch you."

My eyes fell closed at the sound of his voice, my entire body coming painfully, vibrantly to life with the need to *run*. He was still in the ReGen room. His voice was not much more than a whisper, for he didn't need to speak loudly for me to hear. A whimper escaped me at the idea of him catching me. I'd done the one thing, the only thing, that would guarantee this wasn't over. Instead, it was just beginning as I'd tempted the male in him with a challenge he would neither deny nor resist.

I'd fled. To a Hunter courting his female, I'd thrown down the ultimate challenge. I had run, dared him to catch me...no, *demanded* he catch me, prove himself worthy.

He would follow.

Clenching my thighs together, I realized my instinct to flee was a female Everian's instinct to challenge a potential mate, require him to prove himself worthy. Force him to dominate in the hunt.

It was a mating dance of sorts. I'd called to Quinn's inner beast, if he had one. I was his mate. I was here. I was fleeing. And he would find me and claim me and make me his.

He had not been able to do anything a mate would normally do when I'd transported to the Hive controlled base. He'd been imprisoned. I'd saved him. I didn't doubt he was thankful for it. But now that he was safe, and the ReGen pod healed him entirely, he was taking over. Taking control.

And I'd given it to him.

The chase gave him power.

And on a battleship? It was like child's play. I had nowhere to go. I couldn't run. I couldn't hide.

He *would* find me.

I wasn't sure if I should be eager or annoyed.

When the lift doors slid open and I stepped within, I was both.

"I don't want a mate," I said. Thankfully, the lift was empty or people would wonder why I was talking to myself. But I wasn't. I heard Quinn's chuckle, which had me practically growling in frustration.

"You were tested. Only Atlans in Mating Fever are forced to submit to the matching test. You are *definitely* not an Atlan."

The lift doors opened and I stepped out. Based on the color of the blue stripe on the walls, I was on the engineering floor. I went right.

"My job is at the Academy. I *run* the place. I will not quit."

I heard his heavy footsteps, knew he was now on the hunt. For me.

It was like Hide and Seek and he'd given me a count of one hundred before he started his search.

"I can live anywhere, female. Anywhere you are."

His words pleased me and a smile came to my face without permission. Damn him for being so charming. I came to an intersection of two corridors. I went left. My pace quickened. "Stop trying to charm me, Hunter."

"I saw your hard nipples. I know you are aroused. Run, mate. Hide. I will find you."

The testing came back to me and I imagined I was in a forest, the wind in my hair, my body on fire as the male I needed got closer and closer. As he caught me, whipped me around, filled me with his...

I whimpered. Quinn laughed.

That sound had me pushing on. He might be able to track me, but I wasn't going to make it easy. Two Prillon warriors came out of a room and I slid in past them, the door closing behind me. I looked around. Mechanicals of some kind. The room was lit by a blue glow, the rows of components covered everything from floor to ceiling. It reminded me of a library—the non-fiction section. Here, there were no books, but units of data storage that made the battleship run. A forest of machines.

At first glance, this was nothing like the testing dream, the one where the female was chased through the forest. But in every way that mattered, it was identical. She'd enjoyed the pursuit, reveled in it. Had wanted to be caught.

Did I?

Shit. I knew the answer. Yes. Yes, I did.

He knew it, too.

"Do you know what I'm going to do to you when I find you?" Quinn asked, his steps even. He wasn't rushing, but taking his time and enjoying this. The taunt. The play.

I licked my lips. I wanted to know.

"I'm going to watch your face as I open the front of your uniform shirt. As my fingers brush over the swells of your breasts. Hear the pace of your heartrate increase. Ah, mate, I hear it now."

I took a deep breath, let it out. Tried to calm my heart, which had started to race. It seemed I liked dirty talk, and he wasn't even in the room. God, what was I going to turn into when he was before me?

Oh, yeah, a pile of goo.

"I can scent your arousal from here. With each step closer, you get wetter."

I did.

The almost-silent slide of the room's door had me sucking in a breath. Holding it.

He was here.

"Mate," he said. This time, the voice was from the far side of the room. "Breathe."

I exhaled.

"Good girl."

I should have been pissed off by the endearment, but I wasn't. It was... reassuring. Gentle. I actually *liked* the praise.

What was wrong with me?

Oh, yeah. I no longer had control of my pussy.

And there he was. He stepped to the end of the row of components, set his hands on his hips and looked at me. Studied me. Waited.

So big. So... male. I could smell him. Pine forest and dark male. I had no idea why I thought that. I felt like a silly commercial for men's cologne on Earth. There was no *dark male* scent. But there was, and Quinn had it.

"You should find your marked mate," I told him.

He shook his head, but otherwise didn't move. "We are matched. You are mine."

"I'm not."

He laughed then. "Not yet."

"I'm a vice admiral. I wear the pants in this relationship."

I watched as his gaze dropped to my legs. I held still all the while I wanted to squirm.

"You state the obvious. I see you in pants."

I rolled my eyes. The Earth slang had been lost on him.

"I won't let you control me," I said next, hoping to clarify.

"Yes, you will," he countered so confidently. He crooked a finger at me, beckoning me to him.

I remained still and stared. I had no exit, not without taking him out in the process. I didn't want that. I *wanted* to climb him like a horny monkey.

He didn't do anything but continue to curl that finger to beckon me.

As if he were tugging a string, I stepped toward him.

The look on his face didn't change. He didn't gloat. He didn't laugh. He just wanted me in front of him.

And so my pussy-led body went where it wanted to go. To him.

His Hunter's arm moved so quickly, I didn't even gasp. It was banded about my waist, and I felt every hard inch of him pressing into me. His head lowered and he kissed me.

I wasn't startled. I knew it was coming. I was no dummy. I was just surprised. Not by being kissed. I was surprised by the kiss.

Holy hell.

Holy. Fucking. Hell.

Soft and gentle, not like I expected. His lips brushed mine, back and forth as if learning the feel of them. When he kissed the corner of my lips, his tongue flicked out. Licked that spot.

I gasped. He plundered. It went from mild to wild in a second. He wasn't just kissing me, *I was kissing him.* My hands were tangled in his long hair, the silky strands wrapped around my fingers.

He tasted of mint and man, hot and delectable. I couldn't get enough.

I wasn't a virgin. I'd been with a few men. But being in charge of the Academy kept me at a distance from males. I couldn't have a fling with a cadet. I wouldn't have a fling with staff. The only time I'd gotten a space one-night-stand in was after an I.C. mission.

It had never felt like this. *Never*. And this was just a kiss.

My uniform shirt was open in a flash, and I felt the cool air on my skin before I realized he'd actually undone the fastenings.

He lifted his head. Stepped back far enough to look me over. My bra was plain white and simple. No lace. No satin. No peekaboo styling. And yet, the way he was looking at my breasts, it was as if I were in the fanciest, sheerest of lingerie.

"Take the shirt off." It was a command.

My hands lifted to obey before I considered the bossy request.

It took a second to shrug the durable fabric off my shoulders and down my arms. It fell to the floor behind me.

He stepped toward me. I stepped back. He did it again and I retreated until I bumped into the far wall. His body pressed into mine, and I felt his hard length against my belly. I wasn't the only one eager to take this to the next level. Our breaths mingled, my nipples bumped his chest with every inhale.

I held still as he undid my pants, pushed them over my

hips along with my underwear. His fingers found my center.

I gasped, then moaned.

"Mate," he growled. Lifting his fingers, I could see my glossy arousal on them and I watched as he licked them clean.

My needy scent filled the air. All noise, all sounds fell away except what was in this empty room and between us.

He spun me about and my hands went to the cool wall to brace myself. Stepping into me, he bent his knees, stroked his pant-covered cock over my pussy and the cleft of my ass.

I had no purchase on the wall, nothing to grip or hold on to. And that prompted me to my control, which I'd left on the floor beside my uniform shirt.

Spinning back around to face him, I said, "I'm a vice admiral of the Coalition fleet."

His jaw was clenched tight, the muscles in his neck taut. The hand on my hip was firm, but gentle. He would not hurt me.

Slowly, he shook his head. "Here, with me, you're my mate. Nothing more. You might be in control out there." He tipped his head to the side, in the direction of the room's door. "With me, you submit."

It was my turn to shake my head. "I don't want that."

His hand was back between my thighs, sliding over my swollen lips, dipping into my pussy once, which had me going up onto my toes, then away. He painted my essence on my lips. "You do. Taste."

My tongue flicked out.

"You want this. Submit here. For me. *Only* me."

He opened his pants, reached in and pulled out his cock. Oh crap. It was big. Long. Thick. Pre-cum beaded at the tip and he gripped the base, stroked it. "Only this."

I whimpered. I *never* whimpered.

With his free hand, he spun me back about, my hands slapping the walls again. This time, I was the one who tipped my ass up, pushed it out.

I wanted that cock inside me. Needed it.

"Good. Just like that, mate."

He didn't wait. We'd only kissed. I was still wearing my bra. We were barely uncovered except the important parts. Yet the foreplay had begun the moment he woke from the ReGen pod in medical.

I was wet. I was eager. I wanted him.

He took me, filling me in one slow slide of his cock deep into my pussy. The hand on my hip tightened, held me still when I wanted to move away. He was big and he stretched me wide, filled me so much that it was almost *too* much.

He growled. Took me hard. Flesh slapped. Breaths got labored. The need grew. Bloomed. Exploded.

Then a hand came down on my ass, spanked me. Hard. I startled, clenched down on him.

"That's for drugging me, mate. Forcing me into that ReGen pod."

It was too much. *This* was too much. Taken, used as a male wanted. It was not an even exchange. He was taking me. Fucking me. Working his cock into me as he needed to seek his pleasure. *Spanking* me in punishment.

I came. I was the one who orgasmed. Who practically screamed with pleasure in a mechanical room of a battleship. Who clenched down on his hard cock because

GRACE GOODWIN

the spanking had actually been hot as fuck. My pussy gripped him so hard it made Quinn grunt, made him thrust one last time and come.

It was only when my head cleared enough to process thoughts that I realized he hadn't used me. Not at all. He'd given me pleasure, assured that I'd come first. Only when I had been satisfied had he found his release.

He'd taken care of me when I'd been vulnerable.

Tears swelled in my eyes as he leaned his body into me, holding me in place against the wall in a full body press. He nibbled on my shoulders, his hands stroking up and down my curves with a gentleness I never could have imagined just a few moments ago. I felt like a glass doll, something breakable. Precious. Fragile.

Shit. There went the tears, scalding my cheeks as aftershocks of need jolted me on the inside, my pussy still swollen, achy. Full.

His caresses left me shattered and vulnerable, more than the chase or the fucking or the orgasm, because it was real. Gentle. Safe.

It felt like love, and fuck me if I knew what *that* was supposed to feel like. All I knew at the moment was that it hurt somewhere deep inside, somewhere deep and dark and buried. My chest hurt and my eyes were leaking. Leaking. These were *not tears*. Not. Tears.

"Gods you are beautiful, Niobe. Let's find a bed. I want to do that again. And the next time, I'll watch your face as you give yourself to me, as you submit."

uinn, Battleship Karter, Officer's Quarters

"WE NEED FOOD," I SAID, ENTERING THE GUEST QUARTERS we'd been assigned. Karter had sent a comm with the location while we'd been... busy in engineering. The small private chamber was comprised of two rooms, a main room with a bed large enough for two Prillons and their mate—plenty large enough for what I had planned for Niobe—and a bathing room. A table and chairs and an S-Gen machine were everything else in the quarters. Besides the view of space provided by a window the length of the room, the room was basic, plain, but all I cared about was the locking door and the bed.

We would only be here for the five-plus hours remaining until Zan awoke. Once Zan was debriefed and battle plans were finalized, we would not be returning.

We'd head directly from the meeting to transport and then to Latiri 4. After that... well, I'd be with Niobe. I knew that. Where we'd live had yet to be determined.

And now wasn't the time for the conversation. Now was the time for touching. Learning one another. Making her mine.

I began to shed my new clothes, letting them fall to the floor. I wasn't modest. Not with Niobe. My body belonged to her now. I would not hide it.

After I toed off my boots and began to peel my pants over my hips, I paused. She was still in the entry. Staring.

I grinned. "Like what you see? I hope so."

"I thought you said we needed food," she replied. Her voice was even. She sounded efficient, not curt.

I grinned. "We do. But if we only have a few hours, we'll eat naked."

Her mouth fell open. Good. I'd surprised her. She didn't seem to be surprised by much of anything. She'd transported to meet a mate, but ended up at a Hive-controlled prison. She hadn't panicked, had barely broken a sweat before singlehandedly saving six fighters—including me—with her skill and know-how regarding the transport system.

"I need a shower," she said and walked right into the bathing room, eyeing my body the whole way. My cock hadn't gone soft after claiming her in the engineering room. She'd barely seen it before I crammed her full. I wasn't small. I had plenty to keep her happy.

"Come back out naked, mate."

The door slid shut behind her and I chuckled, walking over to the the S-Gen machine. What would she like to eat? What were her favorites? I had no idea. I made a few selections, guessing as to what she might enjoy. I'd just set them on the small table when the door opened.

She came out wrapped in the bathing towel. Droplets of water fell from the long ends of her hair. I looked her over, from her small feet, shapely calves, toned thighs.

"Lose the towel, mate."

She'd intentionally defied me, but I saw the wariness in her eyes. I was standing before her, bare and ready to fuck. I might have hunted her down and claimed her, but we were still strangers. The connection was there, but we were... new.

She lowered the towel until it was dangling from her fingers at her side.

"Fuck, mate. You're lovely."

Every pale inch of her was perfection. I'd seen most of her earlier, but now, the blind haze of need wasn't blurring my vision. I stared at her defiant eyes, the tipped chin, her delicate shoulders, lush breasts with rosy-tipped nipples. Then my gaze moved lower over her curved waist, wide hips... and then fuck, the pussy that ruled my world.

I grabbed the towel from her fingers.

"Quinn," she said, reaching for it, as if to cover herself.

I laid it over one of the chairs and sat down on top of the fabric. No way was she getting it back now, and I owed it to whomever stayed in these quarters next not to have my bare ass and balls directly on the chair.

Leaning forward, I took her hand, pulled her so she sat upon my lap. I groaned, the soft feel of her on my thighs... torture. Her drying hair was right there and I nuzzled into it, then kissed her neck, the curve of her shoulder.

"Eat," I said, trying to remain focused on the task at

hand, feeding her, caring for her, learning about her, instead of fucking. But it took every ounce of will I possessed not to lay her flat on the table and take her again. "We must eat."

My words were truth. We'd be out on a mission soon. Going weak, hungry, would be stupid and irrational. Sleep deprived because we'd been busy fucking? Well, there were sacrifices I was not prepared to make... and those I were.

Reaching out, I grabbed a spoon and scooped up an Everian dish of seasoned meat and vegetables. Lifted it to her lips.

She opened her mouth and took what was offered, that delicate tongue flicking over the bottom of the spoon.

"Good?" I asked, watching her chew, then swallow.

She nodded. "I can feed myself, you know."

"This is more fun." I scooped some more of the dish, took a bite of my own. "You are Everian," I stated. She'd told me so earlier.

"Half," she replied, then took another bite.

"Human, I'm guessing."

She nodded as she chewed.

"Did you transport directly from the Brides Testing Center on Earth?"

"No."

I grabbed a piece of the green vegetable for myself.

With the skills she'd shown in the prison, I doubted she'd come from Earth. "Everis, then?" I fed her a bit of a savory tart. She frowned, then scrunched up her face as she chewed, then swallowed.

"Not good?"

"Not my favorite."

"What is your favorite?" I asked.

She listed off a few Everian dishes, then leaned and reached for a piece of cut fruit. Lifting it with her fingers, she brought it to her mouth, but the sticky juices dripped onto her upturned breast.

"By the gods," I whispered, watching the droplet slide down the curve and toward her nipple. Without thinking, I shifted to lick it up, then glanced up at her face.

She was watching me, her eyes now soft and a little hazy.

"Sweet," I murmured, then took her nipple into my mouth.

"Quinn," she said, her voice breathless.

"I know," I groaned. I'd made it my mission to get to know her. To *talk*. Not fuck. I sat back up, turned her so I wasn't tempted by her breasts. Only to be enticed by the feel of her ass against my cock, knowing if I shifted her a few inches I'd be deep inside her. "So, human, not from Earth. Not Everis. Explain."

She laughed then, knowing I was close to the edge. "I grew up on Earth."

"Didn't you feel out of place?"

She stared at me. "How did you know that?"

I shrugged. "Humans are simple creatures. Far from advanced. They're... fragile. I'd think you'd have been faster than your friends, even early on. You could probably hear better. See better. Hell, do *everything* better."

She nodded once. "I could. I felt like a freak."

I didn't know what a freak was, but I guessed.

"When I was fourteen, a group of Hunters came to

Earth on a mission. Heard about me. I broke records for running races through the school program."

Ah.

"They came to see me and knew. The mark on my palm was the ultimate proof for them." She grabbed another piece of fruit—which seemed to be her favorite of the foods on the table—and took a bite. "I wasn't allowed to stay on Earth. No aliens allowed, especially ones who stood out. I had to go with them to Everis."

"What about your parents? Hadn't your father been discovered?"

She glanced at me, then grabbed the spoon from my hand. "My father, I guess, was on Earth for a mission. Met my mom and got her pregnant. I never knew who he was. I never knew he was Everian. Hell, I never knew *I* was Everian until those Hunters showed up."

"Your mother didn't tell you?"

"She died when I was six. I lived in foster care."

I frowned, not understanding, then she explained as I ate. The more I heard, the more I didn't like. The idea of Niobe alone with families who didn't really care about her, who didn't love her, made me angry. She'd been alone since she was six.

But now she had me.

"I went to Everis with the Hunters and I lived with one of them with his mate and children. They were nice. Kind. But I was human, at least culturally. It took me a while to assimilate, but I didn't really fit in. When I was eighteen, I volunteered to be a fighter." She sighed. "God, that was the first place I felt… normal. I loved it. They knew how to use my skills and it felt good. I felt like I belonged." She shrugged. "Needless to say, I excelled. I served in ReCon

76

for years, then began to teach at the Coalition Academy. Now I run the place."

Impressive. It made sense now, her need for control. It also made sense why she needed to hand it over.

"What about you?" she asked.

I couldn't wait a second longer. Instead of responding, I kissed her. Tasted the sweet fruit and a flavor that was all Niobe. My fingers tangled in her hair and I held her just where I wanted her.

"Quinn," she breathed. "Answer me."

"Elite Hunter. Raised on Everis. Good parents. I am the eldest and have six siblings. I have twenty-two nieces and nephews." I turned my attention to her neck, kissing the soft skin there as I gave us both what we wanted. "Assigned to Battleship Karter and Section 437." I ended with a kiss on her lips. I was not interesting. Not in the least.

"You have six siblings?" she asked. Out of everything I said, that was what she picked up on?

Nodding, I slid my thumb over her plump lower lip. I did not tell her there was a twelve-year age gap between myself and the youngest, nor that I had spent much of my youth chasing my younger brothers and sisters, bathing them, preparing food. Our family worked together, as a unit. I had chores. Lots of chores. And among them was caring for my younger family members. Protecting them. Keeping them out of trouble, away from danger.

I'd felt like a father when I was ten. I'd resisted the matching protocol because I was not ready to be a father again. I had come to terms with the fact that a female I was matched to might want children, but to be honest, if Niobe did not care to be a mother, I would be pleased.

77

The need to be a parent had been worked out of me by the time I was fifteen.

"Yes, six. All younger. I'm thirty-eight and I waited until two years ago to be tested. While I love seeing all my siblings matched and happy and making lots of babies, I was content with just watching them."

She looked away, bit her lip. "And now?"

"Now?" I wondered.

"You are from a large family. I assume you want a mate and lots of babies?"

I sensed this was a serious question, so I paused. Considered. "You said before you couldn't give me what I wanted. You believe I want... what exactly?" Taking her chin between my fingers, I forced her to look at me.

"Babies. Lots of babies."

I held her gaze and decided to be honest. "I do not care to have children."

The relief in her eyes, the release of tension in her body gave me pause. "By your reaction, I assume you do not want to be a mother?"

She shook her head. "No. I'd be a terrible mother. I have no idea what a good one would be like. I'd have no idea where to start. And the truth is"—she bit her lower lip and stared up at me—"the truth is, I have no desire to have children. I could not lead at the academy and serve the Coalition as I like to do, if I had children to care for. I don't want to be a mother. I never have."

Based on what she'd told me of her childhood, it made sense. But I knew her, at least well enough to see that she'd be kind. Sweet. She'd be a good mother if she did have a child. But I respected her choice not to. I had no desire to be a father. I only wanted my mate to be happy, to feel whole. If that wholeness came from being a mother, I would acquiesce. But if not? Well, the possibility of having Niobe all to myself for the rest of our lives pleased me greatly.

I was staring at her lip, remembering the taste when she spoke again. "Besides, I'm thirty-six. What on earth is called an Old Maid. My biological clock isn't really ticking anymore. My eggs are old and dried up."

I had no idea what her clock was, or how eggs could be tired. I understood her age. Females older than she was had children. It wasn't unheard of. But she didn't want them. And she worried I would, that she would not give me what I wanted. That she wouldn't be a good mate because of it.

My mate watched me intently, worry and pain in her eyes. Not acceptable. Not when everything about her made me content. No. More than content. Happy.

"I want you, Niobe. I do not want children. I have never wanted to be a father. I enjoy my nieces and nephews. Twenty-two of them are plenty of children for me. Niobe..." She looked at me. *Really* looked. "We would not have been matched if our intentions didn't align."

She must have known that, but doubted. Until now. "You really don't want kids?"

Kids? Wasn't that the Earth word for baby goats?

But judging by her earnest expression, she was referring to offspring, not agricultural animals. Perhaps this was more Earth slang.

"I do not want to be a father. All right?" I asked, smiling.

She smiled in reply. "Yes."

I lifted my hips, pressed my cock into her. "We might not make a baby out of it, but we will fuck."

"Good, because I... want more of you."

"I know," I replied smugly.

She rolled her eyes and I stood with her in my arms, walked the few feet to the bed and dropped her on it so she bounced, her legs flailing. I grabbed her ankles, pulled her to the bottom of the bed, dropped to my knees on the floor, then placed her feet nice and wide, on the soft surface.

"Quinn," she murmured, coming up on her elbows and looking down her bare body at me.

This view, fuck. I'd never get tired of looking at her, legs spread, pussy wet and open, her soft belly, full breasts with tight nipples. The aroused look on her face.

I took a deep breath, breathed her in.

"I wonder if you taste as sweet as the fruit."

I didn't wait a second longer to find out, licking up the seam of her pussy, getting all her sticky juices on my tongue.

"Quinn!" she said again, this time in a surprised gasp. Her hands tangled in my long hair, pulled me into her.

I grinned. "You can't control me, mate."

Those were fighting words to her. She released her grip, then slid to the floor directly in front of me. That smile now was feral, lethal to my senses. She was gorgeous, hair tousled, naked, aroused. Playful.

Her hand came to my chest, pushed. I let her, of course. Lowering to my back on the carpeted floor, I wanted to see what she intended.

Fuck. She intended to grip the base of my cock and take me into her mouth. Suck me like a black hole.

Her mouth was hot, tight. Wet. The suction powerful. Her grip firm, sliding. The devious female had me close to coming. She literally had me by the balls.

She sat up, wiped her mouth with the back of her hand. She was panting and very pleased with herself. I was dying to come, my balls full and aching.

Sweat coated my skin, my lungs sucked in air.

This was a battle of wills. Of who was in control. Who would submit.

"You're mine, mate. I control what happens in the bedroom." I wasn't going to argue on this. It was fact.

But she was. A dark brow winged up. "Oh really?" she glanced down at my cock, hard and rigid, slick from being in her mouth, almost purple in color and throbbing with the need to come.

She was right. When I was practically down her throat, there was nothing I could do but give over. What male could resist such a temptation?

But she was at her most vulnerable when her legs were parted, my mouth coaxing her pleasure from her. She was far from in control.

This wasn't going to be resolved in the next few hours. She'd learned earlier if she fled, I'd hunt. I'd always find her. She would always be mine. I had the rest of our lives to prove this to her, to repeat the lesson over and over until she understood.

For now, we both could hold the power.

"A compromise." I curled my finger for her to come closer. She crawled up my body so she was looming over me, her dark hair a curtain around us. My cock nudged her belly, then slid over her pussy.

"Turn around."

Her eyes flared wide in understanding. Slowly, carefully, she turned, tossing one of her knees over my head so she was straddling my face, hers directly over my cock.

"They call this sixty-nine on Earth," she said, flicking her tongue over my cock.

I groaned, bucked my hips. Not to be outdone, I grabbed her hips, pulled her down so she was sitting on my face. I might be smothered to death, but what a way to go. I licked up her sweet arousal, flicked her clit.

She gasped. "What do you call it?" She took me into her mouth, sucked.

I ate at her like a starving man.

"Heaven," I said. "I call it fucking heaven."

The fight now would be to see who came first.

7

Quinn, Battleship Karter, Command Deck

MY MATE WAS SEATED ON THE COMMANDER'S RIGHT, A place of honor. On his left, another female from Earth, Commander Chloe Phan, leaned back in her chair with her arms crossed. The two females knew one another well, apparently. They had embraced before the meeting began, and spoke freely to one another, using first names.

Niobe.

She was mine, and I stood behind her chair like a jealous idiot as the Prillon captain, Prax, grinned at me like he knew exactly what I was thinking.

I doubted that, for my mind was focused on the way Niobe had submitted to me. Given herself over to me sexually. I doubted this was something she did, dressed or naked, and it had been a first for her. No doubt. I'd seen

83

the flare of frustration in her eyes when I bent her to my will. Oh, I didn't force her. Hell, no. But I knew. My matched mate would need to submit, to have someone take control, to let her mind go free, to give over to the safety of someone else with her worries. Questions. Issues she dealt with every single day, instead getting lost in pleasure.

And Niobe had done it beautifully. She'd resisted, at first. I wouldn't have imagined her doing anything less. And her submission had been so much sweeter for it.

Now, seeing her in complete control of herself, her emotions... everything, only made my cock hard. Again. I wanted her again. Still. Why?

Well, why the fuck not? I could scent her. I could scent *me* on *her*. Knew my cum was deep inside her. Marked her, filled her.

Now, in this room, she would know she belonged to me. She could give orders to the warriors here, yet her pussy would ache from the way I'd pounded it with my cock.

She could walk away from the meeting knowing I'd be there to keep her safe, to let her bare her soul to me—clothed or not—and I wouldn't let her down.

Yeah, all that shit went through my head while I should have been following the conversation. About the plan to go back to Latiri 4, to that same fucking hellhole, and save the other warriors trapped inside.

Instead, I was consumed with the knowledge that Niobe—no, the *vice admiral*—was going to be on the mission with us. Carrying a weapon. Putting herself at risk.

In fact, when Commander Karter had respectfully, and

carefully, suggested that she remain on the ship until the fighting was done, she had glared at him until he shrugged and returned his gaze to the battle plans laid out in graphic detail on the table before us.

She and I had been on his ship less than a day and he'd already learned she wasn't going to give in to his commands. I didn't care if she pushed him, but she wouldn't push me. *No fucking way.*

Zan, the huge Atlan who'd tried to kill me, was our primary source of intelligence on the Hive operation going on down there. While I'd been in a cell right next to the transport room, he'd been deep inside the base, spent several days fully integrated into their Hive mind. He'd been put in a ReGen pod to heal. After that, the doctors had spent several more hours removing Hive tech from his body piece by piece. He was in control now, the influence of the Hive gone from his mind, but they'd never really be gone completely. Already the Commander had mentioned transporting him to The Colony once this mission was over.

I expected Zan to argue, but the pain in his eyes was one I'd seen before.

He was dangerous on a good day. Now, with Hive tech scattered throughout his body? There was no way any of us could know what would happen when we went back down there, when the Nexus was close. And we *would* get close to that Nexus because he—*it*—was our mission objective.

Then again, there was no way for me to know how I would react either. The injections that blue bastard gave me had burned like acid in every nerve and muscle... inside my mind. The buzzing noise in my head had been consistent and powerful, and I had no way of knowing what would happen once I returned to that base.

The doctor said my body was at eighty-five percent saturation. Did that mean my head would start buzzing again the moment the Nexus was close? Or had my weakness been lack of sleep, food, water? Would my mind be clear now that my body was healed? Or would I have to grit my teeth and fight through it?

I would, there was no question, but I preferred not to have the Hive buzzing around in my head like insects.

Zan and I were in the same uncharted territory. He'd have lasting emotional effects from his time in captivity, as I would, but he was here, ready to fight, ready to save others. To kill every fucking Hive on that planet.

I only wanted to kill one.

Nexus 4. He'd told me his name. He spoke as an individual, controlled everything on that base. He'd killed the rest of my Elite Hunter unit. He'd tortured my friends and forced us to listen to one another's screams. He'd killed them one by one until I was the only one left.

Karter might be talking about the group mission, but mine was specific. Personal. *Nexus 4.*

I'd have his head before I came off that rock. I needed to know he was dead. Gone. The buzzing in my head had been *him.* And with the doctors unable to remove the microscopic tech he'd injected into my body, there was a very real possibility that once I returned to the base, I would hear *him* again.

In fact, I was counting on it. It was as if he'd put a beacon inside me that would lead me right to him. And while his plan had been to keep me by his side, to fight *with* him, I would use it now to end the fucker.

I paid attention to the battle plan as much as I needed to. I didn't like knowing Niobe would be among us, but according to the plans, she would be implanted with a group of Atlan warriors, fresh fighters from the battleship eager and willing to avenge their brothers still strapped in prison cells.

According to Zan, there were at least a dozen more Atlan Warlords still imprisoned inside the base. So Commander Karter—no, *Vice Admiral Niobe*—insisted we transport in two Atlans from the ship for every one potentially integrated Atlan Warlord.

Thank the gods, the doctors on board this ship had managed to save him. Our Atlan, Zan, knew where the guards would be, where the Hive's most heavily armed soldiers would resist, and where the rest of the prisoners were being held. He was most likely destined for The Colony, but not before we finished this mission.

We needed him. *He* needed to finish this.

The Everian Hunters, like me, had been kept separate on Latiri 4, per Nexus 4's instructions. That's why I hadn't seen anyone else once they'd walked past my cell from the transport pad. Why only I knew of the other Hunters' deaths.

Zan didn't know why they'd separated us from the other prisoners, and I didn't either. I was pretty sure I didn't want to know. I did, however, hope the blue bastard was trapped down there—because my mate had locked the place down before we transported out—with the rest of them. He had tortured me, effectively murdered my friends. If I understood the latest Coalition reports correctly, the Nexus were believed to be the elite leaders of the Hive, their commanders and organizers. The brains that ran their entire operation. They were a unique species, conquering and integrating the rest of us to use in their war.

One had even tried to create a female mate for himself. Or so I'd heard. That rumor hadn't been in any official reports, but I had contacts on Rogue 5, and according to them, the female in question—a human like my mate—had not only escaped a Nexus unit, but managed to set a trap and kill him. The very idea made me want to go rip heads off like an Atlan beast.

When that specific Hive Nexus had died, thousands of integrated warriors had dropped dead on the battlefield in several nearby sectors of space. The scientists on Rogue 5 believed that most of the fallen had died from the shock of such an abrupt mental separation, but some had blinked, looked around and woken as if from a nightmare.

I'd asked around, within the Coalition, but the Intelligence Core was tight-lipped about the Nexus units and what they did—or didn't—know about the Hive leadership. They didn't share information, because the Nexus had spies as well.

My mate was tracing her finger along the map projected onto the table, laying out priorities for extraction.

The first was to save any warriors currently inside the medical labs where the integrations were installed. That area was closest to the transport room, and next to where they'd held me. That transport station was on the third level, deep underground. Before Niobe's arrival, it had not been well defended.

We had no idea what we'd be dealing with this time around, which was why an entire attack force was going to hit the base at the surface in a full-frontal assault. Fighting ships, Atlan and Prillon units on the ground, charging the landing bays and exterior doors.

ReCon teams, led by Commander Chloe Phan's primary mate, Captain Seth Mills, would transport directly inside Level One and attack from the inside.

Chloe sat between her mates, Seth, the human, who would lead the ReCon teams. Her other mate, a Prillon warrior named Dorian, would be on the outside leading a squadron of fighters providing aerial cover, in case the Hive attacked.

"Dora and Christopher will remain here with me," Lady Karter said. The commander's mate sat at the far end of the table and held Chloe's gaze as the two women shared a look I understood well. A vow, Erica to Chloe, to care for Chloe's children should all three of them fall.

"Thank you, Erica." Chloe blinked hard. Based on what I knew of human females, I assumed she was fighting tears. Her mate, Seth, placed a hand on her arm, just for a moment. The touch didn't linger and I understood. Like me, he could not afford to undermine his mate's authority in front of the others, but he also could not ignore her pain. I knew how their collars worked, connecting them emotionally. Chloe was a commander, equal in rank to Commander Karter himself, though her rank came from the I.C., and not the Coalition Fleet's traditional—and bloody—selection process.

She was no less respected for not bleeding in an arena.

In the seat on Erica's right sat a Prillon warrior I'd never seen before, but the insignia on his collar made his rank that of commander as well.

By the gods, I doubted there had been this much rank

in one room outside of Prillon Prime's war room in years. Three commanders, an Elite Hunter and a vice admiral?

The Prillon was inspecting my female, his gaze intense. Interested.

"Why do you not simply supply your transport codes to us, Vice Admiral?" The Prillon's question was nearly a growl.

"Who are you?" I asked. If I needed to, I could have his throat slit before he'd leaned back in his chair, one of the perks of being Hunter swift. Unlike an Atlan, I was subtle, fast and deadly.

"I am Commander Zeus."

Chloe, Erica and Niobe all turned as one, the look on their faces one of confusion. "Zeus?" My mate's voice held more interest than I liked. "How did you come by that name?"

The commander dipped his chin toward my female. "My second father is human, from a place on Earth called Greece. He named me after a human god who threw thunderbolts at his enemies."

Niobe grinned, as did Chloe. "Fascinating. Is your father's name Kronos?"

Zeus frowned. So did I.

"Is your father still alive?" she asked. "I'd love to meet him."

"He is not. My mother, alone, survives. She is on Prillon Prime, protected and cared for in my absence."

Enough. "Commander Zeus, why are you here?" I asked.

Commander Karter cleared his throat. "Commander Zeus has taken command of Sector 438."

"Battleship Zeus has replaced the Varsten." Chloe

supplied the information to my mate as if Niobe would know what she was speaking about. I had no doubt that she did. The Varsten had been destroyed by a Hive stealth ship and its destruction was still under investigation. We hadn't been able to track down the remaining Hive ships.

That's why my unit of Elite Hunters had been requested. I'd been on more Hive controlled planets, inside more caves and abandoned ships than I cared to remember. And nothing had been found. No plans. No rumors. No hint of where the new technology came from or where the Hive planned to deploy another stealth ship. No clues about when or where the next deadly attack might come. When the next battleship would be blown into space dust.

My only job in coming to Battleship Karter, and then transporting down to Latiri 4, had been to track that threat. Find out more information. Hunt down the source so the Fleet could eliminate the new Hive weapon.

I'd failed. My unit had failed.

Not only had we failed, we'd led the Hive Scouts right back to the base where we'd been stationed. I'd had long hours in that cell to think, and the only conclusion was that the Hive had followed us back to the underground base, that *we* were responsible for the deaths of the coalition warriors who'd died defending the base. That I was responsible for the suffering of those still underground.

My team of Elite Hunters.

Somehow, the Hive had tracked us. Predator became prey. And we were taken down.

My only chance to atone for my failures was to save

those who were left and then remove that blue Nexus bastard's head from his body.

"Let's focus on the mission." Vice Admiral Niobe's suggestion was a command and everyone in the room felt the authority in her voice. They sat straighter, smiles fading.

My cock hardened and I had to blink to focus on her words instead of her soft, feminine scent floating in the room.

"The transport system on Latiri 4 is under my control," she said. "I will transport in with the first wave of Atlan Warlords—led by Warlord Zan—and coordinate the attack from the transport room on Level Three."

"I don't understand, Niobe. Why? You should coordinate from here, on the command deck with Commander Karter." Chloe asked the question and I was grateful. I didn't understand my mate's insistence that she be in the first transport.

Niobe shook her head. "The transport system is locked to my DNA. Either I am in the initial transport beam, or no one goes. Once we arrive, the transport room will remain locked down until I give the system my authorization codes."

"A DNA lock? I didn't know that was possible." Captain Seth Mills, Chloe's mate, sighed the words as he leaned back in his chair, arms crossed.

I'd heard of such a thing, but never seen it used. Until she'd rescued us.

My mate had locked down the transport in such a way that only she could get anyone—literally *anyone*—in or out. According to what I was hearing, Prime Nial himself would have a hell of a time trying to override her lockout.

"Damn, girl. That's badass."

Erica, Lady Karter, smiled at Chloe's words, but said nothing. I wished I could see Niobe's face. Was she pleased? Bored? Irritated? Her shoulders were tense, as was the line of her jaw, but that was all I could sense from where I stood behind her chair like a sentinel.

I did not understand Chloe's reference at all. Niobe's ass was perfect. Round. Soft. Very, very female. But as my mate did not protest, and Commander Karter's mate looked pleased with the words, I said nothing. Earth slang was going to be a struggle.

The time alone with Niobe had not been enough. The hours we'd shared were precious to me, but I wanted more. Needed it. She had a past, a history I had barely glimpsed and had yet to understand. Even though she was half Everian, her words, her world, were foreign to me. There was too much about her I did not know or understand, and I needed to know *everything*.

My hand tightened on Niobe's shoulder and she absently reached up to entwine her fingers with mine. That was all I needed to pull me back to the present, to the battle plans. To *her*.

"Once the Warlords give me the signal, I'll transport in the Prillon warriors," she said, her hand returning to her lap. And the vice admiral was back. "The aerial assault should provide the distraction we need to draw their attention and the bulk of their fighters to the upper levels. The ReCon teams will be responsible for capturing the elevators and holding them in the event we need an alternate exit."

"We'll take them, Vice Admiral. I promise you that," Captain Mills assured her, and I believed him. He was an experienced warrior, a tough fighter, and everyone on the Karter respected the hell out of him. I'd been around here long enough to know that.

"Good." Niobe nodded at him, her finger pointing to the schematic of Level Three. "Meanwhile, I'll transport in directly to Level Three with the Atlans. Zan will lead a group of warriors to the prison cells. The doctor has equipped us with knock-out gas. Since we don't know what condition the prisoners will be in, we'll anesthetize them all, slap transport beacons on them while they're still unconscious, and transport them directly to The Colony."

"Piece of cake." Commander Chloe Phan spread her small hand wide on the translucent surface of the table, staring at the graphics on display beneath.

I searched my memory for the word, sure my NPU, the Neural Processing Unit every member of the Coalition had implanted at birth, had malfunctioned. *Cake* was a baked food on Earth. What did baking human food have to do with this mission?

"Where are we going to get that many transport beacons?" Prax asked. The Prillon had been one of the lucky ones, on Latiri 4 for less than a minute, and that time only in the transport room. He hadn't been integrated or tortured, but he had known what was coming. He wanted to save as many fellow fighters as he could. "The Fleet hordes them like precious gems."

My mate stirred in her chair. "Leave that to me. I've contacted Helion at I.C.H.Q. and he assures me the necessary beacons will arrive on the Karter within the hour." The new Prillon commander, Zeus, had crossed his arms and was scowling at everyone, including my mate.

His face was lined with cuts, one large one that had yet to heal.

I'd heard of the Prillon custom of fighting in the arena, and that they chose not to use ReGen pods to heal, instead wearing the marks of battle like badges of honor, proof that they'd earned their place in the Prillon chain of command. I thought the idea interesting, but stupid. The fight? Fuck, yes. I loved to fight. But I had no problem using a ReGen wand to heal. I didn't want anything to distract me from focusing on my mate's body instead of my own.

I didn't like him. He seemed like an ass. A hard-nosed, uptight, Prillon asshole.

My mate cleared her throat. "In regards to the Nexus, he is to be taken alive and brought to me. Under no circumstances is he to be injured. Find him and bring him to me. That's an order. Are we clear?"

Everyone at the table nodded, but I saw the anger in Zan's gaze, knew it was mirrored in my own. I understood orders. I respected the chain of command, even though, technically, I was not part of the Coalition Fleet—more like a hired contractor. But what she was asking? Impossible. The Nexus had to die.

"He has to die, Vice Admiral."

She tensed beneath my hand and sat forward, pulling out from beneath my touch on her shoulder. "And he will, but not on Latiri 4. Have I made myself clear?"

A chorus of yeses sounded.

Commanders Karter and Phan nodded.

I disagreed but wasn't about to try to argue with her now. Not here, in front of all these people. Alone, with my cock buried deep, I could get what I wanted. Vengeance.

In the meantime, I had some questions. "What is knock-out gas? And do you mean *Doctor* Helion? And what is H.Q.?" Another human word I didn't understand?

Commander Chloe Phan, human, grinned at me, her gaze locking with my mate's for a brief moment before she answered my questions. "Sorry about that. Earth slang. Knock-out gas means it will make the prisoners unconscious, so we can transport them without a fight. And H.Q. is slang for headquarters. You know, Core Command."

I knew what Niobe's pussy felt like gripping my cock. I knew what she sounded like when she came. I knew the color of her nipples, but I was beginning to realize that I had no idea who she really was.

iobe, Transport Room, Latiri 4

SURROUNDED BY TWENTY ATLAN WARRIORS, HALF OF THEM partially transformed into their beasts, I couldn't see over the closest set of shoulders as the first round of fighting took place. I lifted my hand instinctively and tried to shove the giant warrior aside.

That accomplished nothing. He turned and growled down at me. He wasn't in beast mode, but his eyes were too bright. He was holding on by a thread... to protect me. So all of his angst and beast rage wasn't directed at me.

"Do not move, Vice Admiral. Warlord Zan will signal when it is safe for you." The Atlan speaking was one I did not know, not that it mattered. They were here to rescue their Atlan brethren along with the rest of the prisoners still alive on this base. Most of the prisoners here, according to Zan, were fighters from Battlegroup Karter. Friends. Family. This wasn't a random ReCon mission for these fighters, this was personal. I was vital to their mission. I got them all here. Until I reversed the lockdown on this base, no one was getting off this planet unless I allowed it.

Hive or Coalition.

Prisoner or warrior.

"My apologies," I replied with a deferential tip of my head. "I served almost ten years in ReCon. It was instinct."

The Atlan nodded in understanding and turned back around to face the corridor, where sounds of fighting still filled the air. I stepped back and tried to be patient as the screams and ion blaster fire filtered back to me through the warriors blocking my view. Not big talkers, the Atlans. Which was just fine with me. They got shit done.

One moment we'd been standing on the transport pad on Battleship Karter and the next we were inside the Coalition's former reconnaissance base, under half a mile of solid rock. Back where all this started. Had it all happened in one day?

God, Rachel and Kira were going to freak when they found out all that had transpired. They'd expected to contact me to hear about sexy times. Oh, there had been some of that, but the rest? This Hive clusterfuck? Totally unexpected. And all of it had happened because I'd been tested and matched to Quinn.

We were back and trapped now. Intentionally, because there was nowhere for the Hive to run, not with the transport system and operations on lockdown. I'd trapped them inside, sealing the doors, communications and transport controls with the Intelligence Core codes I had never really believed I would need to use.

Not that it would matter if the Nexus here could communicate with the other Nexus units via some kind of psychic, internal broadcasting system. We had no way of knowing, and that was why Doctor Helion had comm'd me with new secret orders just moments before the assault began. I was to take that Nexus alive—that was nothing new. But he'd upped the ante. I was to take the Nexus alive... *at all costs.* I was informed, in no uncertain terms, that it didn't matter how many warriors I had to sacrifice to make that happen. I was to lie, cheat, steal, kill or lay down my own life to make sure the Nexus was transported to the I.C. scientists. Obtaining that blue fucker was imperative to ending this war.

Besides those orders, Helion transported two beacons directly into my temporary quarters. Even Commander Karter didn't know I had them. He knew, of course, that we had orders to take the Nexus alive. But he had no idea exactly how far Helion was willing to go to capture him.

I knew the I.C. wanted the blue bastard, but that comm had shocked me. They didn't just want the Nexus, they were willing to sacrifice hundreds of warriors' lives to get their hands on him. *Alive.* That was the caveat. He had to be alive, fully functional. No damage. No injuries. As Helion had informed me, "Not a scratch on him."

Our last lead on a Nexus had been on The Colony months ago. A Forsian renegade from Rogue 5 named Makarios and a human female who had—unknown to us —been altered to become the mate to one of the Nexus units, had vanished in a stolen ship. Much to Helion's aggravation, the Fleet had been unable to track them. They appeared and disappeared like ghosts.

Damn Rogue 5 pirates and smugglers. No doubt that Forsian pilot knew every hiding spot and dead zone in the system. He and his new mate, Gwendolyn Fernandez, from Earth of all places, were using that ship to take out small Hive outposts. One after another. It reminded me of the *Millennium Falcon* from *Star Wars*. A ship battling the Dark Side.

I'd read the reports. Not that I didn't appreciate their efforts, but they'd gone rogue, beyond the I.C.'s control, and Doctor Helion did not approve of hotshots or soldiers who didn't follow orders. Part of me wanted to pump my fist into the air every time I read another report about Gwen stirring up trouble out here. But the vice admiral side of me agreed with Doctor Helion. We could accomplish so much more with them if they'd just come in and coordinate their efforts with ours.

Attempts to reach out to them had been answered in one, succinct sentence.

We will not be caged.

I had no doubt Helion assured them that no such thing would happen if they just turned themselves in.

That was a lie, of course. They'd be caged and trained, set free only under strict control of I.C. Core Command, and most likely one at a time, to assure compliance.

Doctor Helion was ruthless, but I understood his rationale. It wasn't one planet, one species, one solar system at risk in this war. It was all of us. When that fact tipped one side of the scale, there was nothing capable of balancing out the equation. Nothing he wouldn't risk or sacrifice to defeat the Hive threat. And that meant getting this Nexus. Alive.

A few hundred warriors from Battleship Karter were nothing to him, to the overall success of this never-ending war, not when we had a Nexus within our grasp.

"Clear." A deep voice filled the room with a roar and the five Atlans who had formed a solid wall of protection around me stepped away so I could take in the damage.

The Hive had definitely been expecting an attack. Instead of three integrated Viken manning the transport room, six integrated Prillon warriors lay on the floor around the transport controls.

I didn't know if they were dead or unconscious, and I wasn't going to ask. I had bigger fish to fry. I needed to unlock transport on Level One so Quinn and the rest of our assault team could get inside.

I checked my wrist. "Three minutes until ground assault."

The Atlan who'd been standing in front of me grunted. "We'll be finished by then."

I grinned up at him. I couldn't help it. "Find the Nexus and alert me at once. Do you understand? No one touches him without authorization from me."

"We heard the order, Vice Admiral." The Atlan transformed in front of me, growing taller, broader, his jaw elongating, becoming thicker. His smile was menacing now. Frightening. I ignored the display.

"He's mine, Warlord. Spread the word. Anyone touches him and I'll have their balls in a sling on my belt."

His bellow of laughter rolled back down the hallway as I moved to the control panel and removed the lockdown on Level One transport. I comm'd the Karter, knowing my mate would be listening from his position on a transport pad on the battleship. Worrying.

"Karter, this is Vice Admiral Niobe. Transport three has been cleared. Recovery of prisoners is underway. Level One lockdown has been removed. You are free to transport."

"Casualties?" Commander Karter's voice was clear. Controlled. But I knew he wasn't asking for himself, but for the rest of his crew. They had family down here. Sons and mates. Brothers.

I looked up at one of the three Atlans who had been left behind to guard me—and the transport pad. "Warlord?" I asked.

He lifted one of the Prillons from the ground and placed him on the transport pad. "So far, none. We are saving as many as we can."

There was pain in his voice, resignation I more than understood. We'd all lost friends in this war. "Zero casualties to report. Operation ongoing."

"Understood. We are initiating transport to Level One. Aerial assault incoming."

"Understood. Prepare The Colony to receive incoming warriors."

"What shape are they in?"

As if *that* wasn't a loaded question. But Karter knew I wouldn't lie or sugarcoat the truth. I looked over the third Prillon placed on the transport. He was covered, head to toe, in silver. However, the warrior next to him had little to show for his time with the Hive but some implants on his forearms. "Varied. Some of them are fully integrated. Tell Doctor Surnen he might not be able to save them all."

"Understood. Karter out."

"Niobe out." I watched from the control panel until Quinn's group had successfully transported to Level One. They would clear the area, then make their way down to Level Two. The Atlans would get the prisoners off this floor, move up the single elevator to Level Two, and we would meet the Level One assault team somewhere in the middle.

That was the plan.

Only problem was, we had no idea where the Nexus was—or what he was truly capable of—and that could change everything.

I motioned one of the Atlans to my side and placed his palm on the biometric station, scanning him into the system. "This transport is yours now, Warlord."

The other two paused, one dropping the last of the six Prillons onto the transport pad with a loud thud. "What are you doing, Vice Admiral?"

"I am leaving you three in charge of this room. I have some hunting to do." Perhaps it was my imagination, or wishful thinking, but I could *smell* him now. The Nexus. His stench had been all over my mate when I released him from the cage I could see now across the corridor. I hadn't known what I was scenting at the time, but when Quinn had told me about his time in this place, I'd connected the dots.

Quinn would be hunting him as well, eager for vengeance. The order to take the Nexus alive had been given to everyone on this mission, but I knew my mate. I'd seen the need to kill in his eyes, and I couldn't blame him. Not really. That creature had tortured Quinn, killed his friends and made Quinn watch. And Zan, I didn't know what the Atlan had planned in his own mind.

The Nexus deserved to die, and *accidents* happened on the battlefield all the time.

But not this time. And with the Nexus 's scent filling my head, I knew he'd been here, and not long ago.

For the first time in my life I felt like a true Hunter, an Everian. I felt my father's blood flowing in my veins and the thrill of the hunt pounding through my body. I wasn't afraid of my gifts. I didn't feel like a freak. I felt powerful. Unique. Special.

Because of Quinn. Because he accepted me as I was. Desired me without even knowing a thing about me. Wanted me. He'd *hunted* me.

And for the first time in my life, I was hunting with a true purpose of my own. I had someone to protect. Someone I cared about.

Someone I loved. Quinn.

This time, it was personal.

That blue bastard was mine.

uinn, Latiri 4 Subterranean Base, Level Two

THE NEXUS CROUCHED OPPOSITE ME, HIS DULL, BLACK EYES impossible to read. There was no expression there, no response to pain. He did not telegraph his movements, the claws protruding from his fingertips long, curved and sharp as any blade. He was nearly as fast as I, an Elite Hunter.

But not quite.

Which was why a cut on his cheek bled dark blue, the color bringing a smile to my face as we slowly circled one another. I'd drawn first blood, and I was in no hurry to finish him. This kill was mine and I'd take my time with it, just as he'd taken his time with me. He'd tortured the Hunters under my command and made me watch, forced me to listen to their screams, kept me weak and helpless in my cell while he killed good warriors that I'd grown up with. Trained with.

They'd been brothers in truth, if not in blood. My brothers. My family.

A circle of silent warriors surrounded us. There was no cheering, no taunting from the other fighters who had transported here with me. Not only had I personally survived torture at his hands, but my mate had set us all free. Not literally, but if not for my mate, *my female,* Commander Karter would not have known the Hive had overrun this base, and every warrior we'd come back to rescue would have been lost forever.

My mate had bought me the right to this moment and the warriors surrounding me would not deny me this kill. Nor would they try to stop me, despite our orders. They knew. They understood.

This fucker had tortured *our friends,* our *family*.

We'd been here less than an hour. The attack had been swift, the plan having gone perfectly. We'd all come together, fighters from different backgrounds but with one purpose. The mission was considered a success. Every contaminated, integrated, captured Coalition fighter had been transported off this rock to The Colony, or to a medical station on board the Karter. I didn't envy the doctors their jobs, deciding who to try to save, and who was too far gone. Watching warriors' bodies disintegrate on the table when their Hive implants were removed. Or telling their loved ones that they could never return, that they'd been banished to live out the remainder of their lives on a rocky planet far from home.

Why some survived the removal of their Hive implants and some did not was, as far as I knew, a mystery.

This blue bastard in front of me probably knew, but I wasn't interested in talking to him, only in making him bleed. Die.

I heard the elevator doors slide open, followed by murmurs as the fighters who'd been on the other levels continued to arrive. At least a dozen Atlans stood surrounding us now, silent statues with one purpose—to make sure the Nexus never left this circle.

If I didn't kill him, they would tear him to pieces.

I.C. wanted him alive. We all knew it.

But this was personal. He was *ours* right now. And he would be ended.

"Why do you waste time, Everian? Your games are inefficient." The Nexus questioned me with a voice void of all emotion. I doubted he understood taunting, but that's what it was. His dark blue patchwork flesh appeared to be held together by strands of silver, a monster bound by shimmering thread. Except that thread *moved* like living serpents winding and twisting through his flesh. The movement was slight, slow, measured. I doubted any but a Hunter would see the subtle shifts between the assortment of blues that created the appearance of a face, but the effect took any hope of normalcy from him. Did he even *have a face?* Or was that patchwork created for this galaxy, just for us? What was he beneath the uniform and metal and strange blue flesh?

Whatever the Nexus might be, he was not one of us, a living, breathing entity with a soul. He was *other.*

The oddity increased when I observed that, despite the past five minutes of intense sparring with an Elite hunter, the Nexus was neither winded nor showing signs of pain.

He bled, but did he *feel?* Did he care if he lived or died? Did he have any emotions under that hideous blue skull?

"I'm going to kill you." I stated my intent as calmly as I could. A fact. Nothing more.

"Repeating threats is also inefficient." He truly did not seem to care whether he lived or died, which only made me want to make him suffer. But would he suffer? I didn't know, but it was definitely going to happen.

"And all the integrated fighters you lost today?" I asked.

If he could shrug, he would have. "Easily replaced. Water-based organisms of your type and size are plentiful in this part of the universe."

This *part* of the universe? Fuck. Were the Hive not just in our galaxy, but others? Just how far did their threat spread? Every planet had a different name for our galaxy. The Coalition Fleet assigned our galaxy a number. But to fighters like me, to the innocents living on the planets we protected, this galaxy was simply home. Coalition space.

"What do you find in other parts of the universe?" Sick fascination stayed my hand. I was speaking to one of the Hive minds, one of their leaders. I was no longer chained in a cell. I was not one of his water-based organisms now.

"We have integrated a multitude of other life forms."

What. The. Fuck? "Like what?"

He tipped his head as if assessing either the sincerity of my interest, or the reasoning behind my question. "You primitive life forms would not be capable of understanding the complexity of the others."

Primitive life forms?

Gods, he was evil, arrogant. And *slow.*

I moved with no warning, giving the opposite side of his face a matching mark.

When I was finished with him, he'd be bleeding from a hundred cuts.

Then I'd kill him. I grinned, narrowed my gaze, ready to inflict more.

"Enough! What is going on here?"

I froze and the Nexus turned his head in the direction of the perfect female's voice. My female. My mate. The look on his face made my blood run cold. Not fear. It was as if he'd been *waiting* for her.

"Stay back, Niobe. He's dangerous." I yelled the warning over my shoulder, afraid to take my eyes off my prey. He wasn't as fast as I, but he would be impossible to stop if I didn't see him initiate a move. Even surrounded by Atlans.

"Move," she snapped and the ring of fighters parted.

My mate stepped forward to stand shoulder to shoulder with two Atlan Warlords, chin high, a look I'd never seen in her eyes.

No. I'd seen it once before, right after she killed those three integrated Vikens the first time we'd been here— right before she'd set me free.

"Warlords, please take the Nexus unit into custody and bring him to me."

"No. Niobe, no," I told her.

Her eyes flashed with fury as they met and held mine. Every Atlan in the circle had responded to her order, closing in on the Nexus like a seven-foot wall of power.

He wasn't going anywhere.

And Niobe wasn't going to let me kill him.

Turning away, I caught Zan's gaze and held it long enough to be sure he understood what I wanted.

His slight nod let me know he not only knew, he agreed. I could go talk to Niobe in private, convince her that what I needed—what *we all* needed—was right. The Nexus had to die. Now. In front of all the fighters he'd tortured. In front of the fighters whose brothers and fathers and families he'd hurt.

Zan took my place in front of the Nexus as two other Warlords moved into place, restraining his wrists and ankles. Our enemy was trussed and ready for delivery to the vice admiral in less than a minute.

"Zan, hold him here," I said.

"Yes, sir." I didn't outrank the Atlan, but I didn't really have a place in the Coalition's pecking order. Elite Hunters were special operatives, given a lot of latitude in what orders to follow, and who we had to report to.

But that freedom did not go to Niobe's level. A commander? Yes, under the right circumstances. A captain? I didn't bother worrying about.

But a vice admiral? And my mate? I had to convince her to do the right thing.

I moved to Niobe and leaned in close. "Can we speak in private?"

Her gaze lifted from the blue monster to me and she gave a curt nod before leading me back to the still open elevator box. She stepped inside and closed the door, sealing us inside. Alone.

Her hands lifted to my face and she inspected me with an intensity I'd never experienced, not even from a doctor. Her care, her concern for my well-being was something new to me. Yes, I had sisters who harassed and teased me, but no female had ever looked at me like this.

Like I *mattered*. Like I was an important part of her.

Like she loved me.

Did Niobe love me? My body lit up at the possibility, but I forced it back down. I'd only met her earlier today. Fuck, was that all? And yet, perhaps she did love me. And if she did care, she'd give me what I needed.

I needed to kill that fucking monster outside these doors.

"He deserves to die, Niobe." I stated the fact bluntly and her gaze clouded, her hands dropping from my cheeks to her side.

"I agree."

I sighed. Thank the gods.

"Good. Then this discussion is over. I'll finish him and we can go back to the Karter and get to know each other better." I meant that I'd take her back to the battleship, wash every inch of her curves and then conquer her body until she collapsed from exhaustion. That was my idea of the perfect end of an insane day.

She shook her head. "No. He's coming with me to I.C. Core Command."

I was shaking my head before she'd finished the sentence, my hands rising to wrap around her shoulders. "No. He's mine."

Her eyes narrowed, her gaze deliberately dropping to where my firm grip tightened on her arms. "Elite Hunter Quinn, you will release me at once. You are not to touch that Nexus unit again. In fact, you will remain in this elevator and return to Level One where you will transport back to Battleship Karter to be reprimanded for insubordination."

My blood ran cold as she stared me down.

Fuck. Fuck. Fuck. This was not my mate. This was not the woman who'd wrapped her body around me and come all over my cock. This was an I.C. operative, a vice admiral, an officer in the Coalition who could have me thrown into prison for what I'd done here. But she'd agreed with me. I didn't understand.

I removed my hands slowly. "Niobe..."

Her chin tipped up. "You may address me as Vice Admiral. I am taking the Nexus unit to Core Command, as was ordered by Prime Nial himself, then will return to the Academy in approximately one week. You will turn yourself in to Commander Karter for disciplinary action."

"No. I. Niobe—"

She cocked her head to the side and I realized just how much trouble I might be in... and didn't care. I couldn't—wouldn't—talk like this to Karter or any other superior.

I swallowed hard. "*Vice Admiral*, the Nexus killed my entire unit and made me watch. He tortured me for days. He's singlehandedly murdered thousands of Coalition fighters and even more innocents. He has to die."

She waved her hand and the elevator doors slid open. There was no mercy—no love—fuck, no feeling at all in her eyes when her gaze locked with mine. Like she was a Nexus unit. Emotions on lockdown. "You have your orders, Hunter. I will not repeat myself."

She stepped off the elevator and the crowd of fighters parted like she'd waved a wand and magically divided them into perfect lines. They moved silently, clearing her path to the Nexus who was on his knees, his hands locked behind his back, his ankles shackled, and a black cloth bag covering his head.

Niobe didn't even look back at me. She removed two small transport beacons from her pocket, placed one on the Nexus, one on herself, and one second later, they both disappeared. No floor vibrations or hair raising with that transport.

Zan stood where the Nexus had been moments before, his hands clenched into fists, the muscles on his neck bulging as he fought down his beast.

He'd wanted the kill as badly as I, and my mate had denied us both.

No. Looking around the room of silent, sullen fighters, I realized that she had denied us all. It wasn't until I stepped to the edge of the elevator, stopped, remembered that she'd ordered me to Level One, and to transport back to Battleship Karter for *disciplinary action,* that my heart began to crack into pieces.

My mate... no, the vice admiral... no, *my mate* had betrayed me. Betrayed us all.

I'd had less than a day to win her heart, and I'd failed.

She'd not just denied me the kill, she'd left me behind.

10

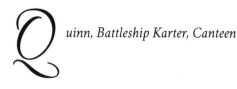

uinn, Battleship Karter, Canteen

"What the fuck are you doing here, Hunter?" Karter said as he approached.

We were in the canteen the floor below the command deck at a table in the back corner. The room had been filled fifteen minutes earlier with those who had finished a shift and with those eating in preparation for one. S-Gen machines lined one wall, windows lined another. Looking out, the universe was as black as I felt. Stars and galaxies spread from one side to the other, reminding me that my mate was out there on one of those bright white specs. Light years away.

The clatter of dishes and silverware were Commander Karter's backdrop. I breathed in the tangled scent of hundreds of meals, not my mate's scent. She wasn't on the battleship. I knew it, not only because I'd watched her transport from Latiri 4 to… somewhere with that blue fucker, but because I didn't smell her. Didn't hear her breathing or her heartbeat. I didn't sense her.

She was… gone. It had been a week since the mission to shut down the Hive prison base. Since then the Coalition had taken back the territory near the base and broken it down. The base was gone, and so was my purpose for being in this sector.

Things had moved quickly. Life moved on. But I hadn't. My mate had been gone for a fucking week. No word. Not a peep. I'd known her for about seven hours… and nothing. My life turned upside down.

"Well?" Karter asked, pulling out a chair and dropping into it. Three low rank fighters just finishing their meals at the table behind ours stood and fled. Clearly, they didn't like the tone of their commander's voice.

They didn't have to worry. It was directed at me.

A doctor in a green uniform approached, handed him a tablet. Karter glanced at it, nodded, and the male walked away without saying a word.

"That's what I asked him an hour ago," Dorian, the fair Prillon who was mated to Commander Chloe Phan, told him. "He's been quietly fuming."

We'd finished our meals; trays and dirty plates littered the table. Zan and Zeus had gone to the machines and retrieved drinks. While I had been given clearance by the Everian council to leave Battleship Karter and move on to a new assignment, I hadn't bothered to check in, to evaluate the options.

I didn't care about earning more money. I was already wealthy. My family, every one of my siblings, mates, nieces and nephews, were well taken care of on what I'd already earned in this war. I was an Elite and we charged a very high price.

But the truth was, there was nowhere I wanted to go, not alone. Without *her*.

Zeus slammed a large cup of alcohol onto the table before me, the dark liquid a spicy brew from Everis. The others sipped a pale colored alcohol from Prillon Prime. Dorian, had something called beer. An Earth drink I assumed his mate, and Seth, the other male in their Prillon trio, enjoyed from their home world.

Slouched in my chair, I had my arms crossed, my half-empty glass resting between my fingers. With my legs kicked out long in front of me, I had no doubt I appeared more relaxed than I felt. I now had an idea what an Atlan felt like if separated from their mate. As if missing a part of themselves. I had no cuffs. I had no Prillon collar. I just felt like half my soul was missing.

I couldn't fucking breathe.

And after only knowing and being with Niobe for... fuck, less than a day? I was screwed.

"It's been days since the battle and he's been like this the entire time. Barely says a fucking word," Zan said, his voice deep.

"Aren't you supposed to be on The Colony?" I asked. If he was going to pour acid on open wounds, so would I.

"I leave tomorrow, Quinn. But Prime Nial lifted the ban on the contaminated returning home." His voice held resignation, not hope. Still, he was a good warrior. A friend.

"I'm sorry, Zan. I'm being an asshole. So, where are you going? You going home?"

He shrugged, the slight movement masking a mountain of pain. "No. They will only fear me, despite the lifting of the ban. I will not belong, and I doubt I'll be matched now. Not like this." He pointed at himself.

"I've heard there aren't many females on The Colony, either. If it's a mate you want, you should go home to Atlan." The Prillon commander, Zeus, offered his advice. "Fuck those who fear you. Let them be afraid."

Zan shook his head, taking another sip of his drink rather than respond and none of us pushed him. This was his life, what was left of it. And when it came to obsessing about females, I had no room to talk.

I wasn't sure what he was going to do. He'd proven himself returning to Latiri 4, but he *was* integrated. Substantially. He *should* go to The Colony. That was the protocol. With Prime Nial's new rules, it wasn't mandatory now. Karter wasn't going to force his transport. But would Zan transition better on The Colony with others who understood his new life? Or should he return to Atlan and take his chances there?

It didn't seem like Karter was pushing him to transport. But, apparently, he was pushing me.

I respected the commander, but in this moment, I didn't like him all that much. For days he'd been fucking with me.

Karter kicked my chair and I held back a warning by biting the tip of my tongue. I was not, technically, under his command. But I knew better than to insult a Prillon battle commander on his own fucking ship. "Leave me be. I'm fine."

"He's barely said anything since the vice admiral transported with the Nexus back on Latiri 4," Zeus explained. Like a recap had been necessary. Everyone knew what had happened. Dorian had been above ground and *he* knew. These ranking fighters were like a bunch of girls, blathering and gossiping. "Days ago."

I sighed.

"Exactly," Karter snapped. His shoulders were tense, his gaze shrewd. Didn't he ever relax? "Like I said, what the fuck are you doing here?"

Seth walked over then, handed a drink to the commander. Karter nodded his head in thanks and took a sip as Seth sat across from me. Five Coalition fighters sitting around drinking and looking at me. Probing me for my inner thoughts and feelings.

What the hell was this? An intervention?

"Commander Karter." A voice came from the leader's comm unit on his wrist.

"Go ahead," he said, lifting his arm to speak into it.

"The data you requested from Prillon Prime has arrived."

"Send it to my comm," he replied.

"Affirmative."

"Sorry, Commander, direct interrogation doesn't seem to be working with this very stupid Everian," Dorian said when Karter was done with his communication.

Dorian was trying to coax me out with humor, a little lighthearted banter to get me to talk. Karter, the opposite.

I took a swig of my drink. This was my second, not enough to get me drunk, which I wanted to be, so I could wallow in my own anger. How many males in the galaxy had their matched mate transport away on their first day together?

Karter sighed. "Fine. I shall handle this a different

way." He pulled his ion pistol from his thigh holster and aimed it at me. Seth pushed his chair back two feet to get out of the line of fire—but the bastard still laughed.

I could see the weapon was set to stun and I rolled my eyes.

"Talk or I stun your ass and take you to Dr. Moor for counseling."

My eyes narrowed at the battlegroup leader. "You play dirty," I countered.

"Don't try to pull that Hunter shit and run off faster than I can blink. I'm a fast shot. I hear Dr. Moor has a couch for you to lie on. Says it helps a patient to relax while they share their feelings." A slow smile spread across Karter's face. "Talk."

It had grown quiet in the canteen, conversations dropped to whispers and no one was eating. I couldn't hear one scrape of a fork across a plate. And I heard everything if I let it in. I doubted everyone had paused to listen me baring my soul. But waiting to see if their commander intended to shoot me? That was high value entertainment.

"Commander," someone called.

Karter lifted his free hand, waved it in the air, but didn't look away from me. He didn't need help.

I sighed. "My answer to your question is, I've been working."

"Why aren't you with your mate?" he countered.

"If you remember, my mate transported off of Latiri 4 with the Nexus."

The Nexus who had murdered my friends, tortured them in front of me, forced me to listen to their screams. I was confident the blue fucker had worked on Zan's integrations, too, but I didn't look his way. This wasn't about him.

"She didn't kill him, didn't end him. She should have let me kill him so that no one else's life could be destroyed by him and his minions," I continued. "She transported him to some... some I.C. base. She saved his life."

"You're pissed because your mate saved the Nexus's life?" Karter asked. He hadn't lowered his weapon. Yet.

I leaned forward, set my glass on the table. "He was mine to kill. He controlled me. Controlled all the prisoners who went through that base."

My sensitive ears heard Zan's deep growl, knew it was his inner beast. He'd wanted the Nexus dead, too. I looked into his eyes, knew it.

"And you think Niobe is yours to control?" Karter asked.

I whipped my head around and glared at Karter. "She's my mate!"

"She's also a vice admiral."

"She's my mate," I repeated, my voice deep, slow, as if that would help them understand. "I want to take care of her, not control her." She was brave and fierce and perfect. I didn't want to change her, I just wanted her to allow me to take care of her, body and soul. She needed release. She needed to let go. She needed a safe place to surrender to the world... to me.

"So you say. And as her mate, you see a part of her that no one else does."

Karter was recently mated to Erica, along with his second, Ronan. Seth and Dorian were mated to Chloe. Both Earth women. Both quite a bit like Niobe because of their shared culture.

"Your mate remains here on the battleship with you. She's not a fighter."

Karter shook his head, lowered his weapon to rest on his thigh, but he didn't slip it back in his holster. "No, she's not in the Coalition in the same way everyone at this table is. Or your mate. But she is Lady Karter now. She is responsible for everyone in the battlegroup *not* fighting. She's the highest ranking civilian officer in the battlegroup, and she takes care of me."

A large task full of responsibility. Full of people to take care of. Women, children.

The commander.

"You want Niobe to remain by your side where you can keep her safe," Seth said to me. He glanced to Karter, then reached for his glass on the table, ensuring he wasn't going to get shot by doing so. "You want her to be with you, within sight, so you can protect her."

"Of course." I looked to all of the males. "You can't blame me. It's in our very nature to protect."

"No, Quinn. It's in our nature to *control.*" Everyone glanced at Dorian who sat across the table. "Our mate is a commander. Chloe works for I.C. Do you think it's easy to let her go off on missions, leaving not only us, but two children behind?"

"Then how do you handle it?" I asked. "Chloe was at the briefing before the mission. She was in control then, just like Niobe. You two were there, allowed it. You allowed her to go into battle with the Hive."

He grinned, looked to Seth. "We didn't *allow* her to be at the briefing. We didn't *allow* her to go into battle. Her superiors require it. Her job requires it. Your mate outranks everyone here. Hell, she outranks everyone in the entire battlegroup."

Seth sighed and shook his head. "We're both captains. Chloe's a commander. Like your mate, she outranks us. She might be ours, but she also belongs to the Coalition. *And* the I.C."

"They don't fuck her."

"Watch it," Karter warned.

Seth held up his hand. "No, it's okay. I understand what he's getting at." He looked to me. "And you're exactly right. The Coalition and the I.C. own Commander Phan outside of our quarters. But within? She's ours, and she knows it. She *needs* us to take command."

"You have the collars. Of course, she knows what you want."

Dorian slowly shook his head. "When she drops to her knees for us, when she shudders with pleasure every time we give her a command, we don't need collars to know she's giving us control."

"Or that her surrender brings all three of us pleasure." Seth tugged at his collar, then stood. "Time to go see our mate."

Dorian grinned. "Damn straight."

They left without another word. They weren't Hunters and didn't move quickly, but they were hustling. No doubt our conversation had them *eager* to see their mate.

"I'm unmated," Zan said. "I tested recently and am waiting. My mate is out there. Somewhere. I am possessive of her now, even though I don't know *who* she is, or where. I understand your concern." He set his supersized forearms on the table. "My beast doesn't, for he wants to go search the galaxy for her right now. But like I said, look at me. I doubt I will be matched now." He paused, moved the conversation back to me. "You were tested?"

I nodded.

"Remember, the testing gives each of you the mate you need, not the mate you think you want," he said.

A member of the engineering staff approached the table, handed Karter a tablet. This seemed to be a consistent occurrence for the leader. "Not three. Only two."

The engineer agreed on whatever the topic was, then took the tablet and left.

Karter couldn't get a break long enough to enjoy a single drink in the canteen. But his female, Erica, accepted him anyway. Loved him. Belonged to him.

There was no question Niobe was my mate. I thought of the instant connection. The heat. The way her body came alive beneath my hands, how her mind went quiet when I took control. Perfection.

"She was doing her job," Karter said, finally tucking his pistol away and taking a big swig of his drink. "She didn't take the Nexus from you just to be hurtful. *It was her job.* Having him in the hands of I.C. scientists could mean hundreds... thousands of Coalition fighters might be saved. Her decisions aren't personal. They're instrumental. Complicated. Difficult."

"She hasn't reached out to me. For seven fucking days."

"I have a thirteen-year-old niece on Atlan," Zan said. "I do not know how it is possible, but you sound exactly like her."

"Fuck off, Zan."

He laughed. "Stop whining."

I glared at him.

"I've been here five minutes and been interrupted three times," Karter said. "This is what my life is like. My time is constantly redirected to things besides Erica. Like, dealing with your sorry ass. A commander's mate understands this. *Erica* understands this."

"Yes, but she is female."

All emotion slipped from his face and he lifted his weapon again. This time, he held it out to me, handle in my direction. "Here, take it. Shoot yourself now before any female hears you speak that way."

Zeus grunted. "It is good your mate is not on the ship. If she truly is Everian, she'd have heard those words from any corner of this ship and did that speed running thing to get here before you could get out the word 'sorry.'"

"You're a dumbass," Zan added, with a shrug of his broad shoulders.

"I'm not belittling women," I said, pushing the pistol away and holding up my hands. "They are smarter, more cunning and resourceful than we are. Hell, an Atlan female could snap me in half."

They nodded.

"But we're males. It's in our fucking DNA to protect and possess. To be in control."

All three were quiet for a moment. Since they weren't countering that, they must have agreed with me.

"Do you doubt your mate's abilities in battle?" Karter asked, head cocked to the side.

I thought of her getting me and the other prisoners out of Latiri 4 when she'd been completely unprepared. She'd expected to find a mate waiting for her, not the fucking Hive. Her involvement in finishing that base. Shutting that Hive shit down. She'd been incredible.

"No."

"Then you must let her fight. Let her do her job," Zeus said.

"Hunter, the problem isn't with Niobe," Karter declared. "It's with *you*. You are mated. Get your head out of your ass. You must compromise."

"Compromise," I replied, as if I'd never heard the word before. "How am I to do that?"

Karter stood, slapped me on the shoulder. "Let her be vice admiral."

What the hell did that mean? "And?"

"She is giving you the opportunity to be you. A Hunter."

I was still lost. The Prillon, Zeus, slammed his huge fist down on the table. "For an Elite Hunter, you are not very bright."

I turned to stare down at him. "I'll take you right now, Prillon."

He had the nerve to laugh. "You are too slow to catch a female who wants to be caught. You are not worthy of a challenge."

What was he talking about? What was I not seeing?

Thank the gods, Commander Karter put me out of my misery. "What does an Everian love more than anything?"

"The hunt." It was in our blood. Our DNA.

"So why aren't you hunting?" he asked.

Realization dawned and hope made my body come back to life. Karter slapped me on the back, a bit too hard.

"As of right now, you're dismissed from this battleship. You can go back to Everis, accept a new assignment, or..."

"Or?"

He grinned. "You can hunt your mate down. Why do you think she hasn't contacted you?"

I just stared at the commander until realization dawned. My mate was Everian. She had instincts, as well. And an Elite female from my world needed not to be courted... but to be *caught.*

11

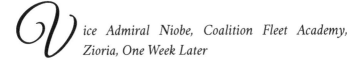

ice Admiral Niobe, Coalition Fleet Academy, Zioria, One Week Later

SO MUCH FOR MATCHED MATES.

I didn't speak the thought aloud. Surrounded as I was by high-level Coalition ambassadors and military commanders, now was definitely not the time or the place to be mooning over one sexy Everian Hunter. Nor should I have spent the last few days micro-analyzing every moment we'd spent together, wondering if I truly would have to sacrifice my happiness for duty. I felt like a high school girl wondering if the quarterback really was interested. Why, now, did I have normal girl feelings? I didn't have time for that stupid shit.

Yet, I still thought. Considered. As for right now, it looked like the answer to the sacrificing was a resounding yes. Which really was not helping me concentrate on this meeting.

My meeting.

Shit.

Cadets had returned to campus the day before and were settling back in. While they were prepping their uniforms, tablets and weapons for the months of classes and training ahead, the staff was an hour into the preterm meeting. The thirty-four head instructors, twelve military commanders from various planets and two representatives from Prime Nial's version of a presidential cabinet were in attendance and we were less than a quarter of the way through the jam-packed agenda.

Twice a year we gathered. The military commanders updated the academy instructors on what they were seeing in the field, recommending changes to the training protocols and getting information from Prime Nial's closest military advisors on what might be coming down the pipeline. Every once in a while, an I.C. commander or scientist would show up and demonstrate a new weapon or advancement in technology.

This meeting spanned several days, none of them short. Every topic was important. While we were steeped in tradition, we also had to adapt to change, to what the Hive was using against us.

I was the facilitator and had to present high-level data on the previous term's cadet training outcomes. Each of the instructors would share the findings of their specific work areas. I might be in charge, but I wasn't a micromanager. Everyone had their tasks, their goals, and were expected to achieve them. If they didn't, this was the meeting to hash out why. The current topic was appropriate stun settings in battle simulations. It was important for cadets to be stunned, to know what it felt like and how to respond to a stunning, but there was a careful balance on success versus incapacitation. I was listening, but I let the conversation swirl around me.

To say I was distracted was an understatement. Ever since I'd returned, I'd been scattered. I couldn't focus. Couldn't get motivated for the new term. It wasn't because of the break. It wasn't because I went to The Colony to visit Kira and Angh. It wasn't because I'd been part of a team who had shut down a secret Hive prison and delivered a Nexus unit—alive—to I.C. No.

That was all straightforward and simple. It was Quinn. Quinn had completely messed with me. Maybe it was that the sex and the orgasms had scrambled my brain, because I craved more. Constantly. It wasn't like I'd mated three Vikens and come in contact with their seed power. God, if that made a female hornier than I was, I felt for her. I'd touched myself, made myself come in the shower tube at least once a day since I'd been back. And another time in bed before I rolled over and tried to sleep. I was a total orgasm slut now. And why? Because I could hear Quinn's voice in my head. *You might be vice admiral in that uniform, but out? You're mine.*

I squirmed in my chair. Subtly, so no one would notice as this wasn't the first time. I was mated. But I was on Zioria and he was on the Battleship Karter. Or I assumed he was. It had been a week. A week! Where the hell was he?

Was taking the Nexus unit from him really so unforgivable? He was a Hunter. An Elite. He knew what was at stake in this war.

And if that wasn't the case, then things were even more depressing. If it wasn't the Nexus, it was simply me.

I'd told him. *Told* him I couldn't be what he wanted. Fine, he didn't want kids either. Great. One hurdle down. But I was I.C. He'd learned that damned quick when I had to take the Nexus unit to Core Command instead of letting him kill it. God, I wanted him to tear that blue monster into pieces. I *wanted* to kill the Nexus unit myself for the torture and pain the big blue enemy had inflicted on my mate. No one fucked with my mate.

Orders were orders, and this war was a lot bigger than one Hunter's torture. Bigger than a few dozen Coalition fighters integrated on that base. For Quinn—and for me— this Nexus unit was a personal enemy, which made things difficult, but getting that Nexus unit to Doctor Helion to analyze might save a thousand more Hunters. Millions of people. Still, I understood Quinn's desire for vengeance, his need to finish it.

The I.C.'s need to study and defeat the Hive trumped a single Elite Hunter's need for justice and revenge.

Being a vice admiral trumped everything else in my life, including having a mate. Looking around, I outranked everyone in this room. I took orders from I.C. command and Prime Nial himself. There were a few admirals who ranked higher than me, but they were generally far from here, either out on the front lines or on Prillon Prime serving on the war council. And this war didn't give a shit I was mated. Didn't gave a shit that Quinn was stationed light years away from me. I couldn't quit, not with so much at stake. I couldn't just up and walk away. Transport to some vacation colony and have sexy times with Quinn until neither of us could walk right.

God, that sounded incredible. I squirmed some more.

The stun setting conversation resolved, and I moved everyone on to the next item on the agenda. One of the representatives from Prillon Prime spoke of a program for elite cadets happening mid-term. A mock battle to take place on the Battleship Zeus.

Again, I tuned the voices out, wondered if my testing match was really just a one-night stand. Because that's all we'd had. Hell, it hadn't even been one night. It had been a day. Less than a day. Six hours of fucking and eating and talking and fucking some more.

"What's your take, Vice Admiral?"

I blinked, stared at the Prillon warrior who was obviously waiting on my answer. All eyes were on me. I glanced at my tablet, at the notes that had been audibly generated and recorded. My brain processed the information at lightning speed. "Five female, five male. Two sessions, not one. Lower the stun rating for the mock battle to three and ensure that vids are sent to I.C. They are always interested in new recruits."

The Prillon warrior nodded, seemingly content with my additions.

"Next on the agenda is—"

"Being introduced to the group."

I spun my chair around at the voice. *Quinn.*

Whispers erupted down the long table at the interruption. At the unfamiliar face… at least to them. For me, the face was *very* familiar. I remembered the long, wheat colored hair, the strong brow, the eyes that seemed to be able to look into my soul. The Roman nose, the full lips. I remembered all of it.

I stared at him, mouth open.

He grinned, ignored everyone in the room and gazed

at me. Took in my uniform, the way my hair was pulled back into a bun at my nape. The way I sat at the head of the table. How long had he been standing there?

I didn't need to ask how he sneaked in so quietly. He was a Hunter. So was I, dammit. I should have heard him. Sensed him. Instead, I'd been lost in my thoughts. *About him.* I breathed deeply. Yes, I smelled him now. I focused my mind away from the meeting and to him. Heard the beat of his heart. I noticed everything.

The Atlan who taught hand-to-hand fighting stood, ready to prove his skills if Quinn were a threat. It was almost laughable because I was the only other Everian in the room. No one else was as fast or ruthless as Quinn. The Atlan might be huge and could rip Quinn's head off, but there was no way he'd catch him to do so.

"Thank you, Warlord," I said as I rose from my chair, holding out my hand to stop him. I moved to stand beside Quinn. "I apologize for the interruption, but perhaps now is the time to take a break."

"You're not going to introduce me, mate? I've come all the way from Sector 437."

The word mate wasn't missed by anyone. In fact, everyone smiled and began talking at once. A few clapped even.

Smiling—I couldn't help it, I was so happy to see him —I turned to the group. "Everyone, may I introduce Elite Hunter Quinn of Everis."

The room erupted into a chorus of greetings and murmurs, no doubt speculating about that word… mate. *Mate.* I wasn't sure if they were so enthused because *I* had found a mate or because it was a happy event. I was pleased to see Quinn. Stunned, even. But he'd interrupted my meeting, messed with my order. My routine.

Prime Nial's lead representative came around the table. "Congratulations, Vice Admiral." He tipped his head at Quinn. "Elite Hunter."

Quinn nodded in response and the Prillon returned his gaze to me. "Vice Admiral, if you wish to excuse yourself, I can lead the remainder of the meeting."

"That won't be—"

"Thank you, Warrior," Quinn said, cutting me off.

I narrowed my eyes. Glared. How dare he! This was my meeting. My work. "I am able to continue and—"

"No, you're not," Quinn said. "The warrior has offered his leadership and we shall take him up on that."

He took my elbow in a firm grip and steered me toward the door.

"Quinn," I hissed quietly, but he didn't even turn to look at me. I knew he could hear me. He could hear my heart beating in my chest. His name as a whisper on my lips, he would hear as clearly as a shout.

Cadets in the corridor stopped and saluted as I passed, but I knew they were wondering why I was being led from my own building.

Once outside, Quinn finally stopped. "Where are your quarters?"

"Now you're paying attention to me?"

He frowned. "I've always seen you."

I huffed. "Seen me, but listened? That was *my* meeting."

He shrugged. "It's just a meeting."

My eyes bugged out. "Just a—"

Two cadets walked past, saluted.

God, this was a nightmare. Word of me being mated was no doubt spreading like it was middle school, not the Coalition Academy. I'd been odd when I was thirteen, and I felt the same way now.

I didn't say more, because I couldn't go back into the meeting. That would stir up even more confusion and talk. I turned and walked toward my quarters. As vice admiral, I had the perk of my own house. It was set back from the main dormitories and classroom buildings, with trees surrounding it. While I didn't share the space, it wasn't large. That suited me fine because I didn't collect things, didn't need much and I lived simply. I was content.

Until now. Now, I was pissed.

"This works," Quinn said, looking around the inside of my quarters. The wood floor, the white walls. Plain furniture. The bed in the other room. "Good, now you won't have to be quiet when I make you come."

"Are you kidding me right now?" I shouted.

He grinned. "There she is."

I looked around. "What the hell are you talking about?"

"My feisty mate."

I pointed to the floor. "You come here, out of the blue, and pull me from an important meeting. To what, argue?"

"I came here for my mate."

I thumbed over my shoulder. "Yeah? Well that was your mate back there in the meeting."

He slowly shook his head, looked me over from head to toe as if remembering me naked. I shouldn't be wet, but I was. Why did I want to strangle and jump him at the same time?

He moved over to me in the blink of an eye, then

slowed, stroked a knuckle down my cheek. My eyes fell closed at the touch, but I popped them open, grabbed his wrist and torqued it. How dare he lure me with sweet gestures. He leaned to the side to alleviate the pressure of the lock, but spun the other way, taking me with him in a circle so he was behind me, his arm about my waist. I felt the heavy prod of his cock against my lower back.

"I came for you." His breath fanned my ear.

"You came to piss me off." I dropped my weight so his arms held me up, stomped on the top of his foot. His hold loosened, and I moved across the room at a Hunter's pace. He didn't follow.

"I came because you're mine." He curled his finger, beckoning me back over to him.

I set my hands on my hips. "You can't pull me out of a meeting."

"You shouldn't have taken away my kill."

My gaze narrowed. "So that's what this is about? You're fucking with my job because I took the Nexus unit away from you?"

"It was my right to destroy him."

"That meeting is my *duty*. We weren't discussing cookie recipes. We were discussing training protocols, changes in Hive fighting strategies, how to keep more fighters alive. Training cadets so they don't panic on the battlefield, so they can hold their own in this war. That's my *job*. That is *my* right."

"I'm your mate. They can plan and gossip without you for a few hours."

"I'm the vice admiral! That was *my* meeting."

His jaw was clenched, his muscles tense. And from across the room, I could see the thick bulge of his cock pressing against his uniform pants. Attraction wasn't our problem. Everything else was.

"I'm not going to repeat our argument from Latiri 4," I said. "You have to understand, Quinn, that my job *is* my life."

"It shouldn't be. You need more than meetings and duty. We are mates. It's my job to take care of you now."

I sighed. He wasn't behaving this way to be annoying. He sincerely believed everything he was saying. Maybe he was too used to operating in a small unit of Elite Hunters with nearly complete autonomy. The Hunters chose which missions to accept and which to refuse. Once on a hunt, they lived by their own code of honor, their own rules. They served the Coalition, and Everis sent regular fighters to the war, but the Elite Hunters were a whole different level. They were not normally in the direct chain of command, didn't report to someone like me. They bypassed the bureaucracy, the red tape. The meetings. I sighed.

"How do I make you understand? No one does, that's why this is so hard. No one has ever understood me. On Earth, I was so different. Everything I did screamed *freak*. Then on Everis, I didn't fit in. I behaved like a human. I didn't like Everian food. I didn't know the customs. So I left. When I joined the Coalition, I finally felt like I had a place where I belonged. Everything I did was accepted. My differences made me better. I understood what to do, how to do it. When, where, why. It was all laid out for me. I thrived. Excelled." I pointed at the shoulder of my uniform. "Vice Admiral at thirty-six."

"And now you have me," he repeated.

I nodded. "I do, but in order for *you* to have *me*, you get a vice admiral, too. Do you know who I report to?"

He shook his head.

"Prime Nial. Who's above him?"

He frowned, then said, "No one."

"Exactly. No one. While there are a few admirals, and Doctor Helion at I.C. Core Command, I report directly to the Prime. Everyone reports to me. Everyone else in the Coalition Fleet is under my direct command. *Everyone.* Think about that."

He crossed his arms over his broad chest, looked down at the floor. When he didn't say anything, I kept talking, blurting more words.

"Commander Karter is in charge of one battlegroup. I'm in charge of training cadets who go to hundreds of battlegroups all over the Fleet. I'm in charge of operations on multiple fronts, including I.C. missions."

"Like the Nexus unit," he said, tilting his head so he looked at me with intense, pale eyes.

I nodded. "Yes. Like capturing the Nexus unit. My job never stops, because the people who report to me never stop. The fight never ends."

"You have to rest sometime," he replied. "You have to take off the uniform at some point."

I nodded. "I do. I did when I was bride tested. It was between terms, and I was on The Colony visiting friends. Then you happened, the whole hot mess with the Hive prison. But now the term is beginning. That doesn't wait because I've been mated. I have a job to do, Quinn. An important job. Thus, the meeting you interrupted."

He shook his head. "I apologize for disturbing your meeting."

I stared at him, wide-eyed. Those words were unexpected.

"But I think *you* need disturbing. You might be vice admiral, but I'm your mate."

I wanted to find the nearest wall and beat my head against it. And I hadn't even brought up the way he'd answered *for me* when the Prillon warrior had offered to take over the meeting.

One fight at a time.

"Quinn—"

"It is my job to see that Niobe, not Vice Admiral Niobe, is fed, rested, safe, happy. Healthy."

"Fine, but I have to get back to my meeting."

"No, you don't. The Prime's guy can handle it."

"But—"

"No. Strip."

I stepped back. "No."

"Yes," he countered. "Strip."

"I heard you the first time." I took another step back.

"Then do as I say."

"I'm too mad to have sex with you."

His pale brow went up. "Oh really?" When he took a deep breath, his nostrils flared. "You're wet."

I was. Damn it.

"You can't boss me around. Drag me out of meetings and tell me what to do."

"I apologized for the meeting. As for the rest, yes, I can boss you around. I can tell you what to do. Take off that uniform, Vice Admiral, so I can see Niobe. I want my mate."

Oh. I wanted him. Wanted sex. God, that hard cock I'd felt… I wanted it in me. Filling me. We could argue all day long, but that wasn't going to get me a single orgasm. Or Quinn's skin on mine. His lips… everywhere. My desire fought with my mind, and since I'd already been dragged out of the meeting, the damage was done. What was the saying? The horse was already out of the barn.

He'd apologized. It was time for me to bend a little. Or strip.

He didn't move, barely breathed as I took off my uniform. Every bit of clothing until I stood bare across the room from him. I looked at him, waited. Watched as his eyes heated, his jaw tensed, his cock grew beneath the pants.

"Show me how wet you are."

His rough voice had my nipples pebbling, had my heart rate picking up.

I palmed myself, slid fingers over my wet folds, then held up my hand for him to see. My wetness glistened on my fingertips.

He shook his head. "Not like that. Turn around. Bend over."

Holy. Shit. He was filthy. And I loved it.

The wood floor was cool beneath my feet. Good thing since I was hot all over. I turned and did as he said, leaned forward so my butt was up. So my pussy was right there for him to see.

He walked over at a human's pace, taking his time to look at me. I watched him, even upside down, watched him look at my very center. Knew it was wet, open. Swollen and ready for him.

Even though I saw him move, when his hand settled on my bottom, I startled.

"Shh," he soothed, stroking his big palm over my skin. "Put your hands on the wall."

He held my hip as I straightened to do as he said. Now, I looked straight ahead at the white wall, my ass out. "Good girl."

"I'll have you know I'm a vice admiral, not a go—"

He spanked me then, one slap to my bottom.

"Shh," he repeated. "I know what you are. Out there, you command. In here, with your gorgeous body on display just for me, you're mine, and you're being very, very good."

I gritted my teeth, willing myself not to wiggle my hips for more.

"Then why did you spank me?" I questioned, glancing over my shoulder at him.

He was fully clothed while I was bare, bent over. Vulnerable. *Letting* him spank me. I should turn around and kick his ass for wanting to spank mine. But the truth was, I loved the sting. The shock of it. I loved letting go, just a little, allowing someone else to be in control.

"Because you need it."

I laughed. "Need it?"

He spanked me again, this time on the other side of my ass. It wasn't hard, but it held a lot of sting. I gasped, then groaned when he drew a finger up my slit.

"See? You need it. Clears your head."

"What are you talking about?"

He spanked me, one side, then the other. Harder. Then slid a finger inside my wet core. I groaned. Yes, that was what I needed. But his finger wasn't long enough, or thick enough. I needed his cock.

He spanked me three times in a row, swift and hot

with that one digit inside, not moving. Heat engulfed me. The sting morphed into warmth, fire. A glow that spread, made my pussy all but melt.

"Quinn," I panted.

"What was your meeting about?"

"What?" I asked, frowning.

"Your meeting," he repeated, then gave me another swat.

"I... I can't think when you do that."

Leaning forward, he whispered in my ear. "Exactly." He stepped close so that his cock and hips pressed into my heated ass through the material of his uniform. Why wasn't he naked?

He moved back and I whimpered, missed the feel of his uniform against my bare skin. The discrepancy between us was so noticeable. Everything was melting away but him. But Quinn.

He dropped to his knees behind me. Breathed, then licked.

"Quinn!" I cried at the touch of his tongue. There, on the entire length of my pussy, then settling on my clit. Flicking it, circling it. I couldn't help shifting my hips, practically fucking myself on his face. My palms pressed into the wall, but they became slick. I could barely keep myself in the right position, but I was so close to coming.

Quinn must have sensed it because he sat back on his heels, then pushed to standing.

"Quinn," I said again, in the most desperate, needy voice I'd ever heard come from my throat. He was turning me into an animal. I turned, faced him, wondered why he stopped.

He walked toward my bedroom, stripping as he went. He turned in the doorway. "Come."

"I was trying to," I grumbled. My nipples were tight peaks, my pussy so wet that my thighs were coated. I was so sensitive, so ready to come all I had to do was rub my thighs together.

The sight of him, naked and... god, incredible. His long hair brushed his broad shoulders. Abs so hard a quarter would bounce off. A cock he used for very magical orgasms. And he was all mine.

I started to go to him, ready and eager for that huge cock, but he held his hand up.

"Kneel."

He went into the bedroom, sat on the edge of the bed so I could still see him. He gripped the base of his cock, stroked it and looked at me.

"Are you serious?" I asked.

"Submit, mate."

There was a soft rug on the floor at his feet where he wanted me to kneel before him. Kneel. Submit. Give him complete control in order to get the good, hard pounding I wanted.

"Niobe," he said when I didn't move. "The only one here to see you give yourself to me... is me. There's nothing to worry about. No one to command. To consider. No orders to give. No meetings to run. I am going to take care of you. Fuck you. Make you come. Make you scream in pleasure. Don't think, just listen to my voice and do as I say."

While I had Everian senses and could hear, smell, see everything in fine detail, it all shut down to just him. His voice. His breath. His words.

We were alone. There was no Academy outside the door. My uniform was a pile of clothes on the floor. The clothing meant nothing without the body to fill them.

Right now, I was just Niobe. Quinn's mate. Could I do this? Could I kneel for him, give over to what he wanted so I was under his power? He was making a point, negotiating the dynamics between us... telling me what he wanted. He was a Hunter, an Elite. Strong. Fast. Controlled. A predator. Dominant by nature. The question was, could I give him control in this? Did I trust him enough to let go? Surrender? Submit?

The human side of me was arguing with everything happening. Indignant. Irritated. Furious that he'd interrupted my meeting. But the Everian half? God help me, she was so fucking hot I was having trouble holding her back. All I could think about was the fact that Quinn had dominated me on the Karter, he'd hunted me down, chased me, fucked me and filled me with his cock as my Hunter's nature had craved from a worthy mate. The Everian half of me was more than happy to give him anything he wanted, now that he'd conquered me in a mating hunt—even on a battleship.

I was at war with myself. Logic versus instinct. Need versus my human idea of the perfect man.

Growing up on Earth I thought I'd wanted someone reserved. Careful. Quietly supportive. We would never argue, I'd thought. Never fight. Never fuck like mindless animals.

Quinn was far from reserved or careful. I knew we'd argue, a lot. And I was on fire just looking at him.

He continued to sit there and stroke his cock. He was as turned on as I, but he was being patient. Waiting. All I had to do was go to him and we'd both get what we wanted. Needed.

"I see you, Niobe." While his voice was deep, full of need, it was calm. Almost... comforting. "I see who you are. What you need. Just for me. Submit. Let me take care of you. Stop thinking. Just feel."

Those last two words held more heat than I could process as I focused on his strong hand moving at a steady pace up and down his cock. I wanted that cock. It was mine.

Slowly, I lowered myself to the floor, got on my knees. Looked up at him. I didn't look away, just breathed and waited, my pussy clenching. So wet.

"You're so beautiful," he murmured. "So perfect." His free hand came up, tugged my hair from the bun so it fell over my shoulders. Unable to wait, I leaned forward and licked the pearly drop of pre-cum from the blunt tip of his cock. Tasted his salty flavor.

He hissed and I knew that while I was on my knees before him, bare and exposed, he was right there with me. I held power over him. No one else could make him buck his hips with desire or feel the need to thrust and fuck. I made him an animal, subject to his base instincts. Just as he made me eager for him. Wet. Ready. Aching to be claimed.

I blinked and the next thing I knew, I was on my back on the soft bed. He'd used his Hunter speed and strength to put me there. He crawled up my body, nudged my knees apart with his as he went.

I looked up at him, all lethal Hunter, but his touch— besides the spanking—was gentle. Reserved. As if I were precious to him. "Gods be damned, Niobe, I don't think I can wait."

I bit my lip. Nodded. My bottom was hot and aching where it was pressed against the bed, but the extra heat only added to my overloaded senses.

Settling one hand beside my head, he pressed his forehead to my stomach. Breathed deep. "I don't scent my cum on you anymore."

He growled, found my center and thrust his fingers into me with no warning. No foreplay. A blatant, aggressive thrust of possession. I gasped, arched my back. Wanted more.

Moving his fingers in and out of my body, he fucked me with them as he spoke. "If you're going out there in that fancy vice admiral's uniform, then underneath, you've got to be covered in me. Marked. Scented." His fingers slipped out and he moved over me, aligned his cock to my entrance. He didn't wait, thrusting deep in one stroke. "Mine."

"Quinn," I whispered, gripping his sides with my knees as my pussy adjusted to his size.

His body covered mine completely, all heat and scent and wild male. He moved in and out of my body, holding my hands above my head as he fucked me so slowly I thought I would die.

"Every time you're sitting in one of those meetings and commanding your troops, you'll know you're mine," he continued.

My pussy clenched around him and I groaned, clamping down, locking my knees behind his hips. God, his dirty talk would be my undoing.

"No one else will ever see you like this."

I shook my head as he began a steady pounding rhythm, harder. Faster. My toes curled and my muscles began to shake as if I were losing control, not just of my senses, but of every muscle and fiber in my being.

He locked both of my wrists in one firm hand and used the other to push my knee wide and out toward the bed, opening my body to his fucking, giving him the angle he needed to go deeper, to rub against my clit every time he bottomed out inside me. He moved with the precision and control of a machine. Fast. Deep. Over and over and over...

"You want to come?"

"Yes." The answer was out of my mouth before I'd fully processed the question. Yes was my answer to him. Yes to anything. I needed him. Yes.

"Ask."

I licked my dry lips, arched up as he drove deep. I was so close, had been since he had his mouth on me where I stood against the wall. Now, thinking of him waiting for me to kneel before him, pushed me to the edge. I loved giving him control. Loved to forget, to only see him. To only hear him. Scent him. *Feel* him. "Please, Quinn. Let me come."

His hand slipped between us, brushed over my clit. "Now."

That was all it took. One word. His command. I obeyed.

And doing so, I sank into bliss. Into pleasure that made me see colors behind my closed eyelids. Made me scream his name. My pussy clenched and milked his cock for all his cum. His cock grew, tightened, swelled, exploded deep inside me. And through it all, he was there with me, his power and control a balm I hadn't realized I needed, but my soul drank him in like I'd been dying of thirst for years.

Trust. This was trust, and I'd never really given myself to anyone else.

The scent of fucking, of his cum, my arousal, was heady. He was right. I was going to smell like him. Feel the sting on my ass, the swelling in my pussy, the boneless pleasure of my release long after I put my uniform back on.

But for now, I reveled in Quinn, in being a woman in love.

In being just Niobe.

uinn, *Coalition Academy, Three Days Later*

MY MATE WAS BUSY. SHE WAS ALWAYS BUSY. MEETING after meeting, disciplining the cadets, and the instructors —meeting with a constant stream of Coalition Fleet personnel fresh from the front lines with reports on new battle techniques.

I'd pulled her into a few locked classrooms, bent her over a desk or two and reminded her who was in charge... but I was beginning to doubt she was really listening to me in that regard.

Wandering the grounds, I watched the cadets' battle simulations from one of the control stations. They were damn good. Accurate. Meant to get the fighters ready for battle, and they did a great job of recreating the environments and terrains the Fleet fought on every day.

But watching cadets scream and shoot and fake kill one another was not entertainment. At least not for me. The sounds hit too close to home, reminded me of things best forgotten. I'd seen enough battle and death to last a lifetime.

I was not Coalition Fleet. I didn't have to be here. Technically, I answered to the rulers on Everis, and no one else. I'd put together a unit and we'd served the Coalition, done our part in the war. But now, thanks to that Nexus unit, every member of my unit was dead. It was just me left, and I could either put together a new Hunter unit, join a unit looking for a member, or I could make a permanent change.

I could stay here on Zioria. But the idea of roaming the grounds of the Coalition Academy like a guest who had overstayed his welcome did not sit well with me.

I didn't belong here. I was accepted, spoken to, but otherwise ignored. I was not part of this machine. This was not my planet, my people, my life.

What I wanted was to take Niobe to Everis. I had a home there. Family. I could tuck her safely into the family estate and take missions as they came my way, knowing she'd be protected and secure while I did what needed to be done.

I was an Elite Hunter. Wealthy. Respected on every planet in the Coalition.

And yet, I couldn't control my own female. Couldn't protect her. Couldn't provide for her, or keep her safe, or watch over her like I needed to. And while I could dominate her in the bedroom, the moment she put the vice admiral's uniform back on those curves, she wasn't mine anymore.

She was *theirs*. Every single living being who transported on or off of this planet required her attention. Needed her to make decisions, keep things operating. And gods be damned, but I was proud of her. Vice Admiral Niobe was a hard-nosed, no-nonsense commander. She didn't take insubordination, rarely showed any emotion, and always... *always*... remained in control.

And watching her do this to herself was making me insane. I knew the real Niobe, the woman who knelt before me quivering with need. The mate who crawled across the floor to me, who begged to come, and wrapped her legs around me, kissed me like she'd never be able to stop.

The two versions of her were at war in my mind, and although logically, I could reconcile them, my instincts were screaming at me to throw her over my shoulder and run.

Elite Hunters were known to be primal. Possessive. Protective.

And I had a mate who would not allow me to possess or protect her.

The situation was tearing me in two, and I could see no solution. I would never ask Niobe to step away from her position. She was good. Damn good. The Coalition Fleet needed her.

But so did I. More than half the day she was locked behind closed doors, where I couldn't get to her. Couldn't see her. Being a Hunter was what saved me, for I could still smell her. Hear her heart beating. Know she was well. Whole. Yet still removed. My obsession only grew each time I took her, filled her with my seed, marked her with my scent. Obsessed was too tame a word.

And yet, the idea of retirement, of resigning my duties as a Hunter, living a quiet civilian life did not appeal. I would lose my mind cooped up in Niobe's small house like a pet with nothing to do. Sitting around skulking wasn't in my nature either, but I'd been doing a hell of a job of it the last couple days. I was moody like a growing youth.

I was coming out of my skin, unable to protect her, unable to leave.

So I fucked her. Hard. I gave her the only thing I could, pleasure. Orgasms. Relief, if only for a short time, from her duties to the rest of the universe. And in between? I tried not to rip the head off each and every cadet, instructor or visitor who tried to speak to me. I was too raw to be civil, my need to protect my mate driving me to the brink of an Elite Hunter's legendary self-control.

I'd been on hunts in Hive territory that had been easier than letting her walk away and close her office door on me every day. Every. Fucking. Day.

"Elite Hunter Quinn?" A young cadet jogged toward me from the main administration building where Niobe was—at this very moment—locked inside a room with eight Atlan warlords, discussing Atlan training techniques.

More secrets. More details I wasn't allowed to know, but could hear clearly.

"Yes?" I turned to watch the young male approach. He was Prillon and looked barely of an age to fight. But then, maybe I was just getting old.

"Vice Admiral Niobe issued orders for you to report to transport immediately, sir." He added the sir as a sign of respect, not because it was required by Coalition protocols. I was not, technically, part of the Coalition Fleet. I had no official rank. No Intelligence Core clearances. No right to be next to my mate in her meetings. No right to protect her.

But that's all I wanted to do. Protect what was mine.

"The vice admiral ordered me to report?" She was in command of the entire planet, but the idea still rankled. I was not Coalition. I was not hers to command. She was *mine*.

"Yes, sir. She said it was urgent."

Fuck. My irritation faded instantly. What else was she supposed to tell this cadet? Please go ask Elite Hunter Quinn to come to the transport room when he can? No. That wasn't her way. She was a vice admiral. She would give this cadet an order and not think twice about it. Especially if the matter were urgent. I had to gain control of my emotions where my mate was concerned. I was not rational. Hadn't been since I'd met her. Fuck, I was mentally whining. Constantly. Thank fuck I wasn't an Atlan because if I felt this protective without an inner beast...

"Thank you, cadet."

The young Prillon nodded and ran back the way he had come. Urgent?

My heart skipped a beat with worry and days of raw frustration bubbled to the surface at the thought that my mate could be in danger.

Moving with Hunter's speed, I was inside the building before the cadet had made it halfway down the path. Moving as nothing more than a blur, I sped to Niobe's side, my pulse roaring, my entire body raging with the instinctive need to protect my mate.

"Niobe? Are you well?" My voice carried, echoing off the walls of the transport room as I came to a halt at her side. She stood speaking to a Prillon I had the displeasure of meeting on a prior mission, years past. The sight of him didn't improve my mood. Where he went, pain followed. "Doctor Helion."

The Prillon doctor looked me over for a cold, calculating moment before dipping his chin in a nearly imperceptible nod. "Elite Hunter Quinn. Congratulations on your mating to Vice Admiral Niobe."

That was not what I was expecting, nor did I care to have his well-wishes about anything. Fuck that. I would prefer that he stay as far away from my mate as he could get. And stating her full title back to me? What was that? A reprimand for a child? "What are you doing here, Doctor?"

The doctor glanced from me to Niobe, a question in his eyes. When my mate nodded, giving the doctor *permission* to speak, he did so. His words blunt. To the point. "I transported in to speak with the vice admiral about the Nexus unit she managed to acquire on Latiri 4."

Managed to acquire. Right.

"And?" What had they done to the blue bastard? I hoped they'd dissected him alive.

"I am not at liberty to discuss our findings with you. You do not have the required clearance from the I.C."

And that was that. I looked at Niobe, the apology in her gaze not what I expected as I realized she had no intention of telling me more.

Duty. Rules. Command. Secret clearances and the Intelligence Core. But that look meant she didn't like that he was intentionally being an asshole.

My mate was so wrapped up in regulations and protocol that she may as well have been a machine. But she loved those rules, the structure. She'd said as much to me. The Coalition Fleet gave her a place to belong, to feel confident in her skills and abilities. She needed that order in her daily life just as much as she needed me to provide orders and domination in the bedroom.

But I was an Elite Hunter. We operated on our own, outside of the rules, and this structure and protocol was stifling. Suffocating. Damned hard to deal with when assholes like Doctor Helion were pressing down on me like a mallet driving a spike into the ground, trying to make me conform.

How the fuck was I supposed to protect Niobe when I didn't know where she was half the time? When I had no idea who she met with, what they discussed, or what was going on in her life?

In bed, naked, she was mine.

But every other moment of the day and night? She belonged to them. To *him.* To Doctor Helion and the cadets and thousands more lined up behind them.

Biting down my irritation, I focused on my mate, ignoring the doctor completely. "The cadet said you needed me?" I didn't say *ordered me*. Not in front of Dr. Death and Destruction.

"Yes. I have to go to I.C. Core Command. We're going to transport out as soon as Warlord Gram arrives. I didn't want you to worry when I wasn't at dinner."

Going to Core Command? Where the fuck was that? I didn't bother to ask. They wouldn't tell me.

"When will you be back?" I couldn't forbid her from

going without me. Gods fuck me, I wanted to, but I knew I didn't have the power.

She glanced at Doctor Helion for an answer, and he provided one I did not like. "I'm not sure. Less than a day."

Fuck. Fuck. Fuck. "Can you guarantee her safety?"

He stared at me, but I refused to back down.

"I said, can you guarantee her safety?"

"Quinn." Niobe placed her hand on my chest and pushed, gently, trying to get me to back away from the much larger Prillon warrior. He was big, but he was slow. I could kill him in a fraction of a second.

"Quinn!" Niobe yelled my name and the red haze of protective rage subsided. This was not acceptable. My lack of control was not acceptable. The daily separation between myself and my mate was not acceptable. Not being able to protect Niobe was eating through me like fire burning kindling. One spark, and the Elite Hunter inside me would burn. Protect my mate. That was foremost in my mind.

Her submission was a beautiful thing. She handed it to me like a gift. My ability to dominate eased my challenge with her being the vice admiral, but nothing—*nothing*—would soothe my need to protect.

Doctor Helion turned away, breaking eye contact, putting distance between himself and my female. Thank the gods he seemed to have some idea what I was dealing with because as soon as he was far enough away that my instincts said he was no longer a threat, I could think again. I pulled Niobe into my arms and buried my face in her hair. Breathed her in. Calmed the raging creature inside me that wanted to hunt. To kill anything that threatened her. "Niobe. No. I can't protect you if you leave."

"I have to go. I'll be safe. I promise."

"I'll go with you."

She was shaking her head, her cheek pressed to my chest, but she let me hold her here in a public place. I needed her close. Needed to calm down. To know she was safe. Secure. In my arms. "You can't. We're going to a secure I.C. installation. Less than a dozen people even know this place exists. You have to let me go."

"I can't." I wasn't being dramatic or lying to her. My Elite Hunter instincts literally took control of my body. I couldn't let her go. The creature inside me knew she was going to leave him if I did, and *he* tightened his grip like an animal.

Fuck. *I* was beginning to feel like an animal. A beast. I didn't have mating fever, like a fucking Atlan warlord, but I was losing control, just like they did, because I couldn't protect my mate.

I didn't know how Seth or Dorian let Chloe go off on missions. She was a commander and outranked both of them. While Karter's mate wasn't in the Coalition, she did lead all non-fighter personnel for an entire battlegroup. How did they compartmentalize? How did they not lose their minds? But none had a vice admiral for a mate. I was going insane. It was obvious from my looping thoughts about trying to protect her.

Niobe pulled out of my arms and I held myself still, using every ounce of discipline I had acquired in years of hunting to let her go.

I watched as she walked onto the transport pad where

Doctor Helion and Warlord Gram joined her. I watched as she nodded to the transport tech.

"Initiate transport."

"Yes, Vice Admiral." The transport tech worked his magic.

I watched as my mate, my life, my beating heart disappeared… and I had no idea where she'd gone.

This was unacceptable. It was time to stop complaining and mentally whining. That shit was over.

It was time to do something to protect my female.

13

uinn, Prillon Prime, Prime Nial's Personal Study

SECURITY ON PRILLON PRIME WAS A CHALLENGE. I'D HAD to sneak past no fewer than seven guards, and incapacitate two more, to reach this room. The guards would wake up later with massive headaches but be no worse for my passing.

I wasn't on Prillon Prime to cause trouble or hurt anyone. The opposite, in fact.

And I would speak to Prime Nial whether he agreed to a meeting with me or not. I'd tried the diplomatic route, without success. It seemed a lowly Everian Hunter did not simply request a meeting with the most powerful ruler in the known galaxy. I'd been informed, in no uncertain terms, that he was *busy*.

Well, fuck that. I didn't have time for busy. My mate

was out there with Doctor Helion doing gods knew what, alone. Without her mate for protection.

Without me.

So I helped myself to one of Niobe's—no, the vice admiral's—individual transport beacons.

They could punish me for that as well, if they wished.

Or they could try. They'd have to catch me first, and based on the status of Prime Nial's current contingent of warriors, they'd need three dozen more to have a chance. At least. I was not just an Elite Hunter, I was here to protect my mate.

They'd have to kill me to keep me from protecting Niobe.

Looking around the inside the Prime's home, I moved like a shadow. I could smell two males in the residence. One in close proximity to a human female I assumed must be their mate, Jessica, from Earth. The other? Anger and frustration scented the air, his body's response to stress clearly evident, at least to me. The scent came from a small room near some sort of library, ancient historical tomes and heirloom armor lining the walls.

His father's armor. His grandfather's. Marked and scorched and burned in battle. The Deston family was legendary among the Prillon people, and I had no doubt Prime Nial would be a warrior to be reckoned with. But I was more than up for the task.

Moving toward the door, I opened it slowly, knew I'd find Prime Nial within. Alone.

Prillon wood gleamed on the floor. Large windows showed spectacular views of the city below and would serve their leader as a reminder of all those he governed from within those walls. And the male himself... seven feet tall, broad shouldered and powerful.

I made no sound, still he froze with his hand midair over a report and looked up but did not move otherwise. He took his time inspecting me, looking me over from head to toe, assessing my intentions. He had good instincts, setting the report aside and raising his brows at me with impatience. I liked him as soon as he spoke.

"Who the hell are you?" Prime Nial's voice was a quiet rumble.

"Elite Hunter Quinn, Prime Nial. I apologize for the condition of your personal guard." Below, I heard the other male move and wondered what had given me away. Then I remembered the Prillon mating collars. One moment of alarm in Prime Nial would alert his second to danger, to come to his aid, to protect their mate.

While Prime Nial might be measured, reasonable, I'd heard that his second, a beast of a warrior named Ander, was feared among the people, that he carried deep scars from the war and put fear in Nial's enemies.

I wasn't afraid of Prillon warriors, or their scars. Still, I was not an idiot. I needed to hurry. Facing Prime Nial alone was one thing. I had no desire to state my case to anyone else. Ander was irrelevant to my mission.

I remained standing as I waited for the Prillon ruler to decide what to do with me, not wanting to add to my level of disrespect. Breaking into his home unannounced was enough to merit severe punishment. But nothing they might do to me would stop me. I'd already been in the worst hell in that Hive controlled base. A Coalition brig would be like a vacation in comparison. And Niobe was worth any risk.

He walked to stand in front of his desk, having already assessed me for danger and clearly finding me free of any to his person. I wasn't sure if I should be insulted he found me non-threatening, or reassured that the reputation of the Elite Hunters preceded me, and that Prime Nial would assume I meant him no harm.

"I am aware that Elite Hunters are quick, but to get past my guards…" He shook his head and sat down on the edge of the grand desk. I had no doubt he had a contingency of protective warriors nearby. But if I intended to kill the Prime, I would have done so already. "How many did you go through?"

I did a mental calculation. "Nine."

"Alive?"

"Of course."

He nodded. "Impressive."

I didn't say anything, for it was an odd time to thank him for the compliment.

"Should I be impressed, or should I fire my security team?"

My presence here was not the fault of any of his warriors. "All due respect, Prime Nial, but I am an Elite Hunter with nearly twenty years of operational experience. Your guards were unconscious before they even realized I was here."

His non-integrated eye—his left was completely silver from Hive integrations—widened. "Why are you in my home, Elite Hunter? Explain, and it better be damn good."

"My mate is Vice Admiral Niobe."

A smile softened his serious expression. He stood immediately and came forward to slap me on the shoulder. "I had not heard of the match. Congratulations."

I nodded and smiled in return. I *was* pleased and I was not afraid to share that.

"But that does not explain your illegal and unauthorized entry into my home, nor your unauthorized transport."

"Actually, sir, it does."

He dropped down into one of the two chairs that were meant for visitors. The less than formal location eased the worry that I would be escorted away before I put in my request.

"This, I want to hear." He indicated the chair beside his.

Because we were both tall—he much taller than I—the chairs were too close together. I pushed mine back before I sat. "You are mated." I glanced at his red collar. "I assume you are fiercely protective of your mate."

I didn't state it as a question, for if I had, I would be insulting not the Prime, but a mated Prillon male. Not smart.

"Fiercely. Lady Deston is my world. And Ander's."

"How would you feel if your mate was a vice admiral, and part of the I.C.?"

He rubbed his jaw, studied me. I could see why he was Prime. He was thoughtful, analyzing. Considerate, but most likely ruthless. The description sounded a lot like Niobe.

"She is very important to me, to the Coalition." His words of praise for my mate raised my hopes that he would cooperate with my demands.

"She's I.C. She's a commissioned officer in the Coalition. She works with Doctor Helion on a number of highly secretive programs." I spoke as if he didn't know this.

"I see." The Prime leaned forward, his elbows on his knees where he sat, assessing me. "You can't protect her as you wish."

Smart, too.

"I assume you are aware of what happened on Latiri 4, of the vice admiral's capture and transport of a Nexus unit?"

"Yes. That is highly protected intelligence, but as you were there, I cannot fault you for the knowledge."

"I was there. That fucker tortured me for over a week, killed my unit and made me watch."

He sighed and I realized I had lost focus, if only for a second.

"I am sorry about the loss of your unit."

I nodded. There was nothing else to be said. "As I was the only one to survive, I am... between assignments. My unit is gone. I have more than served my time for Everis and the Fleet in this war. Niobe—Vice Admiral Niobe—is not just my mate. She is my job. My *mission* now."

"You are an Elite Hunter, Quinn. You are not one of my officers. You are not, technically, part of the Coalition. What is it you want from me?"

"I want to be permanently assigned to Vice Admiral Niobe as her personal attaché. I go where she goes. I.C. Core Command. The Academy. Every meeting, every mission. It's the only way I can protect her."

"You answer to the Everians, Quinn. Not to me."

"Strip me of my Elite Hunter status. Assign me a commission in the Coalition Fleet. Give me the clearance I need to be at my mate's side."

His brows winged up in surprise. "Why should I do that?"

"As I said, my mission now, and until I draw my last breath, is Niobe. Place me as her personal security. Where she goes, I go."

"And if I refuse?"

It was my turn to study him, assess the threat to my mate. He was the means to a desired end, a solution that would make both me and my mate content, but if he refused? "I will find another way, but I will be with her. I will protect her. I have no other choice. I cannot accept the way things are. I cannot watch her go into danger alone and unprotected."

"She is protected by the Coalition, by highly skilled warriors, by trained I.C. assets."

"And not one of them will protect her as I would, and you know it."

He did grin then and I began to relax, to think that, perhaps, I would have my way without further argument.

"You would no longer be part of the Elite Hunter lists. Ever again. You would no longer report to Everis, but to a higher-ranking Coalition officer." When I didn't even blink at those scenarios, he added, "You'd become nothing more than a Coalition fighter at the lowly rank of lieutenant. You are too smart, too highly skilled and trained to accept that kind of demotion. Hell, you'd barely outrank a cadet."

I shrugged. "Titles mean nothing. You can call me whatever you wish, I am what I am. My skills and training will not change. I am an Elite Hunter, even without the title. No one can protect my mate like I will. I must serve Niobe. But to do that, I need the rest of the Coalition

Fleet to acknowledge my status as her protector. I will gladly follow her commands...."

"And mine." His demand was clear, uncompromising. But I had faith he would not ask anything of me I could not accept. He was not an unreasonable male.

"I accept."

The silence lengthened as we stared at one another, neither of us blinking. His silver eye was uncanny. Strange. But I had no doubt he saw everything. Perhaps more. "You break into my home, incapacitate my warriors, demand to speak to me, and you think I should reward you by giving you exactly what you want?" he countered.

"Yes." I held his gaze, willed him to understand. "Listen to me. I can deal with her being a vice admiral. She's smart, skilled. I do not doubt her abilities or her wisdom. I am proud of the rank she's achieved. I am proud of her, proud to call her mine." I sighed, tried to relax my tense shoulders. "But I can't accept her being in danger. The idea of her going off without me there to keep her safe is making me insane." I leaned forward in my chair, knew a challenge was in my eyes. I would not back down, not on this. This was my future. My mate's safety. "Commission me. Make me a Coalition officer. Give me the highest level clearance needed to be by her side. I am loyal to my mate, to the Coalition of Planets, to the survival and safety of all member worlds. I have more than proven myself. I will not betray you or the Fleet. I would never betray her. Assign me as her personal security. I would be the most highly skilled and ruthless lieutenant ever seen in the Coalition."

"As I said, you'll lose your Elite Hunter status." That statement meant he was still considering it.

I shrugged. "With all due respect, as I said, I don't care. Make me a lieutenant and assign me to the Academy, to her personal security. Where she goes, I go."

"And if I don't?"

I leaned back in my chair. "As a mated male, what would you do if you were me?"

He studied me closely before raising his wrist comm to his mouth. "Security code Nial, Prillon Prime..." He rattled off a string of Prillon code words and phrases before some kind of computer system answered his call.

"This is the Central Core, Prime Nial. How may I be of assistance?"

He looked at me. "Last chance to change your mind."

"Not happening. She's mine."

He was grinning as he spoke. "Elite Hunter Quinn of the planet Everis is hereby enlisted as lieutenant in the Coalition Fleet and shall serve in that capacity until further notice. His security level clearance is to be matched to that of Vice Admiral Niobe of the Coalition Academy on Zioria. He is assigned to her personal security detail until further notice and reports only to the vice admiral or myself."

No lowly officer to order me about as I'd originally assumed.

"Understood, Prime Nial. The lieutenant will be contacted at once to set up clearance codes and access to Coalition assets. Is there anything else I can do for you?"

"No, that will be all."

"Yes, Prime. Have a good evening, sir."

His comm went dead and less than a second later, my

wrist comm pinged. I glanced down, shocked to see the access codes and links to my new position in the Coalition Fleet already in my comm system. I was a lieutenant now. I would go where my mate went. Protect her. Forever.

"You will owe me a favor, Elite Hunter Quinn. An off-the-record favor."

I nodded. "Anything you need, just ask."

Satisfied, he slapped his hands on his huge knees just as a loud bang sounded on the door. "Nial? What is going on in there?"

Ander. It had to be, and he sounded less than pleased. And then I heard the female voice, and the scent of a human female, so similar to Niobe's, came to my attention. I'd been so focused on my discussion with Prime Nial that I'd been ignoring my surroundings, counting on the closed door to keep out the rest of the world.

"Nial? Are you all right? Who's here? I want to meet him." The female laughed, the sound bringing a soft smile to the Prime's face as she continued. "Whoever he is, he's a badass. He took down the entire perimeter guard on the north side of the house and both guards outside the kitchen."

The door opened and there stood the ugliest Prillon warrior I'd ever seen, a huge scar marring more than half of his face and neck. His size, even for a Prillon, was impressive. He was larger than Prime Nial, and his mate's hand rested on his arm with a tender familiarity I missed. I followed that feminine hand to see a gorgeous female stood next to him. She had long silken hair and a mischievous sparkle in her eyes I had become all too familiar with the last few days.

Earth, apparently, had a healthy supply of feisty, independent females.

I remained seated as she entered, sure the position would put both of her overly protective mates more at ease. As she approached, Nial leaned back in his chair, signaling his second that I was not a threat.

Not that their lovely mate gave the possibility a second thought as she came close and perched on the arm of Nial's chair to look me over.

I grinned at her. I couldn't help it. She reminded me of my mate, of Niobe, with her sass and obvious confidence. "Lady Deston, it is a pleasure to meet you."

"Oh, and you are handsome, too."

Ander growled. Nial chuckled. "Jessica, taunt Ander any further with your appreciation for this Hunter—lieutenant now—and he may spank your ass later to remind you who you belong to."

She smiled at her scarred mate where he hovered near me, keeping me within arm's reach... just in case. Him, I understood. Lady Deston, however, was completely unrepentant as she focused her attention on me. "So, who are you and why are you here? Nothing this exciting has happened in ages." She glanced at Ander, then back to me. "How many warriors did you take out?"

"Nine."

"Nice." She looked over her shoulder and down at her primary mate, the leader of the entire Coalition, the military commander in charge of the entire war effort. "You need to work on security around here, I guess." She chuckled. "He took down Hart *and* Tarzan."

"His name is Torzon."

"Whatever. He totally needs to change it. He's got Tarzan vibes all over the place."

Who the fuck was Tarzan, and why was Lady Deston acting so strangely? As if she knew me well, as if I were part of her inner circle. Trusted.

"Mate." The Prime's warning fell on deaf ears and I assumed it was the loving glide of his hand up and down her back that encouraged her to ignore his rumbled warning. I also realized that her treatment of me would change drastically if her mates were not present to keep her safe. She treated me as a friend because she was safe to do so.

And Ander's massive hulk standing so close reminded me of that fact every time I dared adjust in the chair.

Lady Deston looked to me. "Well? Who are you? Why are you here? I want details."

"I am Lieutenant Quinn of the Coalition Fleet, personal attaché to Vice Admiral Niobe."

"Oh, she's a hard case. I like her. She reminds me of Warden Egara on Earth."

"Who?" I had no idea who this Warden Egara might be, but if she was anything like my Niobe, she had to be an amazing, desirable female.

"Never mind. So, *Lieutenant*, why did you sneak in here?"

"Because your mate refused my more polite request for an audience."

"So you took out nine guards and ambushed him at home?"

"Yes, I did."

That made her smile widen with understanding. "Let me guess, this is about your mate."

When I nodded, she leaned into Nial's touch. "All you alpha males are so predictable. So, who is the lucky lady?"

I wasn't sure she was lucky in her fate to be stuck with me, but she would be loved. Protected. "Vice Admiral Niobe."

She froze. "Oh my god. Yes! Finally. I have to call her." She leaped up from her perch and moved to me, leaned down, kissed me on the cheek. Before Ander could protest too much, she moved into his side, cradled there like a treasure... which she was. "I am so excited. I love her. We'll have to come visit. Right, Nial? We can go to the Academy and visit them soon, right?"

"Of course, love. Anything to keep you happy."

Ander led her away, and I grinned as I watched them go. When I turned to Prime Nial, it was to find him watching me. Understanding passed between us.

"The vice admiral was raised on Earth," he said, but I knew what went unsaid. His mate was from Earth. Passionate. Intelligent. Strong-willed.

"Yes, and her father was an Elite Hunter. She is fast. Strong. Wild."

He chuckled. "Go. Get the fuck out of here before I change my mind." He shifted in his seat, his hand going to his cock to adjust it in his pants. "Leave, Hunter. Ander is busy reminding our mate who she belongs to, and I would join them."

It was my turn to laugh as I placed the transport beacon back onto my chest and pressed the button that would take me home. *Home.* To her.

Niobe.

14

N iobe, Coalition Academy, Ziorian Forest

Hunt for me.

The three word challenge I'd left for my mate should have been delivered to him by now. The transport system had notified me the moment he left Prillon Prime. The moment he'd left the Prime to return to me.

I knew what he'd done. The Coalition's core computer system had alerted me to Quinn's new status as a lieutenant in the Coalition Fleet, to his incredibly high level I.C. clearance, and his status as my personal bodyguard.

He would answer to me now. Me and Prime Nial. No one else. Which meant he would escort me from now on. Every mission. Every meeting. He'd be by my side, protecting me, keeping me safe. And when the meetings were done?

Then I'd take off this uniform and submit to him. He would be in command.

The thought made me shiver with anticipation. Need. Somehow, he'd figured out a way to make this work between us without asking me to sacrifice who I was.

It made me love him more.

I was several miles from the Academy. Several miles from anyone. I knew I was alone in the forest. I would hear others if they approached. I would smell them. Being with Quinn had encouraged me to embrace the wild side of my nature, the Everian side. And it felt normal. *Good.*

That, and I knew no one would dare enter these woods because I'd given strict orders that this section of the forest grounds was forbidden until I gave the all clear.

Which meant it was off limits until tomorrow, *after* Quinn and I were finished with the night air, the fresh scent of dirt and leaves and sex.

Sitting upon a fallen log, I waited. I knew the transport tech would give Quinn my note. Those three words would set off the Hunter in him. Knowing he would come for me set something off in me as well. Arousal.

I ached for Quinn. Longed for him. But to say our mating had been easy so far was laughable. Did Kira and Angh have this much trouble? Had there been the Hive and intense battles and possessiveness to deal with?

I was possessive of Quinn. He was mine. The idea of some other female having him, knowing him the way I did—obeying his darkest and naughtiest commands— made my hands clench into fists. I'd pop her in the nose and have her exiled to the outer reaches of the galaxy. I'd send her to a mining asteroid or banish her to Antarctica.

I laughed, the sound absorbed by the forest around

me. I wasn't worried about Quinn returning safely from any future missions. Okay, I did worry, a little. But I knew he was skilled, that wherever he went, he would be part of a team surrounded by highly trained fighters. Bad things could happen. Hell, I'd found him in a cell half integrated. But perhaps it was because of my rank that I accepted the possibility of something happening to him. I didn't like the thought, of course, but I accepted it, as Quinn had accepted me and my role in this war.

I picked at the rough bark on the log with my fingernail. Pulled a piece free and tossed it to the ground in irritation. Sure, he accepted it, but that didn't mean he liked it. In fact, he hated that I was ever in danger. His protectiveness irked me because it scraped against my very human, very feminist sensibilities when he doubted that I could take care of myself. Did he think I'd made it to vice admiral because of a pretty face or blind luck? Hell no. I could fight. I could strategize. I could command. My responsibilities were the one thing I could not compromise on because it wouldn't truly be me doing the compromising; it would be the Coalition Fleet and Prime Nial, the cadets and the warriors out on the battleships fighting this war. I was doing my job to protect what I loved. Earth. Everis. Life.

And Prime Nial was not a Neanderthal. His mate was human, from Earth. And like me, she had a mind of her own, a mind the Prime and his scary second, Ander, respected. Prime Nial couldn't—*wouldn't*—diminish one of his top leaders, male or female, just to please their mate.

Which meant Quinn had to bend or break. There was no bend in me, not when it came to my job.

Surely, Quinn didn't doubt my abilities. He'd witnessed them before he even knew I was his mate. But he was an alpha through and through. It was in his nature, in his very DNA, to be in charge. To control. Protect. Possess. He couldn't handle the possibility of me being hurt because it would be his fault, his weakness, if anything happened to me. *I* was *his* job. Which had left us in a bit of a bind. Until today.

I plucked up a little yellow flower, began pulling off the petals. *He loves me. He loves me not.*

He loves me. I knew it even when he was being so damned stubborn. But going to Prime Nial? Being stripped of his autonomy, accepting a commission and rank in the Coalition Fleet to be with me? That was something I had never expected, nor was it something I would ever have asked of him. He had sacrificed his future and his freedom to be with me. He chose me. He loved me. There was no other explanation.

And I loved him.

"Mate."

The one word startled me, had me almost falling off the log. There, standing in front of me, arms crossed and looking all big and brawny, was Quinn in his brand new lieutenant's uniform. The new look caught me by surprise.

God, I loved a man in uniform.

I raised my hand to my chest, tried to settle my out-of-control heart.

"Should I be concerned I was able to get this close to you without notice?"

I bit my lip to stifle a smile as I looked up at him. The forest was humid, the heat caught beneath the canopy of leaves overhead. It was almost... sultry. Or maybe it was just that my very virile, very hot mate was before me. I knew what was beneath the uniform. All hard muscle, and other *hard* things.

He'd come to me. I may have issued the challenge for him to hunt for me, but my mate had found me. Here. Anywhere. And while he came to me, I would now go the few feet to him.

I stood, tugged up the bottom of my shirt and lifted it over my head as I closed the distance between us. I had my pants undone as I stood before him.

"I was thinking of you," I said.

"Oh? And what were you thinking?" The corner of his mouth tipped up, the only change in his serious demeanor. His stance was still rigid, his chin tipped up.

"Of what you've done."

His pale brow winged up. "And what is that?"

"You gave up your job for me."

His gaze softened and I saw something there I'd never seen before, barely dared to hope for. "You are my job, Niobe. My job is you."

I sucked in a breath, for he'd said the exact words I'd been thinking.

It wasn't all that sexy, but I reached down and tugged off one boot, then the other. When I stood back up, I looked him in the eye. "And like you said, without my uniform, when I'm not vice admiral, I'm yours." I pushed down my pants, took my panties with them. He watched as I toed them off.

"That's right." He still didn't move, only tipped his chin farther to inspect me head to toe. "All of it."

I was still in my bra. In seconds, I had that off and added to the pile on the soft forest floor.

I watched as his pupils dilated and his gaze roved over every inch of my body. I remained still. Waited. He was in charge now. God, the feel of him taking over, of shedding all of my responsibilities like I did my uniform, was exhilarating. I could be more than just the vice admiral. I could just be Niobe, or more importantly, Quinn's mate.

And what he'd done for me... my heart burst and I could no longer remain still. I needed to run, my entire being bursting with joy.

Using my Hunter speed, the gift from my father, I raced naked through the forest, moving so quickly the trees were nothing more than a blur.

He called my name, the sound an agony of arousal. Need.

Hunger.

He'd already hunted me down, found me in the forest. Now I challenged him yet again, roused his mating instincts, urged the Elite Hunter within him to track and capture and claim his mate.

I raced with everything in me, not wanting to be caught too soon, needing to run, to enjoy the thrill of being chased. This was fun. Play, even naked. And as much as I needed Quinn's strong arms around me, his cock filling me, stretching me wide, I needed this, too. So much.

As hard and fast as I moved, I sensed him closing in on me, his nearness like a buzz of electricity over my skin. He was toying with me now, letting me stay just out of reach, playing. Teasing. Making me burn.

His scent filled the forest and I circled around in a

wide arc back to my original trail so I could track his scent, breathe him in with the night and the forest and the singing insects. This was who I was now, with him. Only with him. I was as wild as the animals, as free as the wind that blew my hair from my head in long streaks of darkness behind me.

I felt him seconds before he tackled me, rolling us to the ground, using his body to break my fall.

He was naked as well, and I realized he must have taken the time to remove his clothes, that sexy lieutenant's uniform, to give me a head start.

I flung myself at him, wrapped my arms around his neck and kissed him.

After a second of being stunned by my enthusiastic welcome, his hands settled on my ass, held me to him and rolled me beneath him in the soft leaves, his cock thrusting inside my wet core as we moved.

His cock thrust inside me, making me his, making him mine, and he gave over to the kiss, to the need.

He tasted like… Quinn. Hot, spicy, dangerous. *Mine.* We were both ravenous. Wild. I didn't remember lifting my legs and wrapping them around his waist. His cock was pressed deep inside my pussy. I wanted to whimper and buck beneath him, touch my clit, get myself off. It wouldn't be hard to do, but I resisted. I would let Quinn decide the when and how of my pleasure. That idea alone had me craving him even more.

Our movements slowed to something gentle, tender, and when he lifted his head, our gazes locked. Held.

"Why?" I whispered, studying his face. "Why did you go to Prime Nial?"

"Because I might be part Atlan." He jerked his hips

forward, hitting something dark and needy inside my pussy and I gasped. Groaned. Clung to him.

I frowned. Atlan? That didn't make any sense and I was having a hard time thinking straight with his cock stretching me open. Wide. Full. "What?"

Shifting again, he rubbed his rock-hard abs against my abdomen, shifting his body so that he rubbed my clit as he rode me, plunged deep. "I swear I have an inner beast where you are concerned. I never doubted your abilities. *Never.* I am proud of who you are, mate. Proud that you are mine."

He couldn't stop, his groan of pleasure matching mine as my pussy clenched down on his cock like a fist. I raised my hands over my head and kept them there, arched my back, surrendered.

"By the gods, Niobe." He buried his face in the hollow of my neck, used his hands to lift my hips off the ground, angle me for deeper thrusts. I cried out, lost. I didn't care if he was Everian or Atlan or a monster; he was mine and I needed him.

"Quinn." My voice was barely more than a whisper, but he heard me, the sharp nip on my neck proof of that as I begged to come. "Please, Quinn. I need you. I…"

He stopped moving and I sobbed, but I listened, which was what he demanded of me. "I am proud of you, but I am an Elite Hunter beneath the lieutenant uniform. I am not tame, mate. You brought out instincts in me I didn't know I possessed. I could not control my need to protect you. Going to Prime Nial, demanding to serve as your personal security asset, was the only way I knew to protect you and keep you close to me."

"But your freedom? What about your family on

Everis? Your job?" He was an Elite Hunter, even I knew they were in high demand, and not just for use by military commanders. Private rulers on many worlds hired them for various jobs. They were rare. Valuable. Their services cost a fortune and they chose whom to serve, and whom not to.

By accepting a commission as an officer in the Coalition Fleet, he was now under Prime Nial's command. The Prime could send him on missions, order him to obey, and if Quinn refused? He'd be sent to the brig. Imprisoned.

He slowly shook his head. "I spoke to Prime Nial. His mate is human, like you. He understands what I am dealing with."

I gasped, ready to defend all women of Earth, but he nuzzled my neck and pulled out, thrust forward. My protest turned into a shudder of pleasure as ripples moved through my pussy. He was huge. Stretching me. Filling me up until I couldn't breathe, let alone think. "Can we finish this conversation later?"

"No. Listen to me, Niobe, and understand. From now on, my job is protecting you. Caring for you. Being with you. I don't give a shit about rank. Prime Nial and I came to an understanding. I answer to you, mate. I take orders from you when we are in public. You and no one else."

"Me?"

"You." He nibbled his way to my lips, each kiss melting my heart a little more. "Prime Nial has given me top level clearance, including within the I.C. I go where you go. No questions, no arguments."

I lowered my hands and buried my fingers in his long,

golden hair. Silk. So soft on something so hard. And strong. And mine. "Okay."

That made him chuckle. "Okay? No arguments?"

"Nope. I am naked, after all. I don't argue with my mate when I'm naked."

"You're right." He lifted my ass, opening me to him. Thrust deep. Deeper. "When you're naked, you're mine."

I smiled, stroked my hand over his hair, cupped his jaw. Felt the rasp of his whiskers. And that is when I confessed the truth of my heart. "I'm always yours, Quinn. Always."

He froze for a heartbeat, as if I'd startled him with my confession, but his body went rigid. Hard. My dominant lover was coming out to play, and I needed him to make me stop thinking and just feel. I simply... needed.

"Put your hands over your head and keep them there, mate." The sharp bite of his command only made me more eager to comply. Like a first day cadet, I didn't have to do anything but follow orders.

I moved into place and he remained still, like a commander of his fighters, watching. Waiting for any breach of orders. I squirmed, knowing if I didn't follow his orders, he'd spank me. And that wasn't punishment at all.

As I placed my hands above my head on the ground, I couldn't miss the outline of his expression in the shadows of the forest. His face was lined with strain, the veins in his neck and temples bulging. He wasn't immune. In fact, he was probably as desperate as me. I moved instinctively, opening my legs, trying to pull him deeper.

"Wider."

I swallowed, moved my knees outwards. More, then

more still. Thank god I was in good physical shape. I'd never been more thankful for flexible hips.

His touch heated my skin. The humidity made perspiration dot my skin. But it was his gaze that burned me up. He could see me, all of me in the darkness.

"Mate, you are so beautiful."

I *felt* beautiful.

His hands hooked my ankles and he pulled his cock free, kissed his way down my body, lowered his head to my aching core. He raised my legs, pushed my knees up toward my chest.

"Oh!" I cried as he licked up my slit, found my clit and put his mouth over it. Kissed it. *Ruled* it. My hips came up, rolled into the delicious contact.

"Quinn," I breathed.

He didn't allow me to come, but stopped well before, teasing me, prolonging my pleasure. Ruling my body like a master. Lifting his head, he looked up my body. God, seeing my arousal coat his lips, his chin… wicked.

"Please," I begged. I ached for him, wanted to be filled with him, to feel the hard press of his body above mine. I wanted to shatter with his cock inside me. To know I was protected by him. Possessed.

Perhaps he liked me to beg, for he acquiesced by releasing my ankles and settling himself at my entrance. The blunt crown pressed in and I looked up at him where he braced above me on his forearm. He held my gaze as he moved. Entered an inch. Held.

"Mate. *Mine.*"

He thrust into me then. Hard. Fast. Claiming me. Making me his all over again.

My head arched back, the feel of him surrounding me, filling me... it was too much.

His groan vibrated from his chest and into mine.

"Yes!" I cried. I wasn't a vice admiral. I wasn't in charge of the Academy. I wasn't on an I.C. mission. But I was where I needed to be. In this moment, I was important. I surrendered to my mate. I *gave* my mate what he needed, and in return, he made me whole.

A hand on my hip had us rolling, Quinn now on his back and I hovered over him. Straddling his narrow hips and his cock embedded deep, I pushed up on his chest, loomed over him.

"Quinn?" I breathed.

His hands settled on my hips, lifted me a little, then let me drop back down. I gasped. He groaned.

"Ride me, mate. Fuck the cum from my balls."

I was on top, could move as I wished. His cock was mine to use as I wished. But what I did pleased him. I clenched down and he groaned again, his hands tightening on my hips.

I shifted, circled, lifted up, then dropped. Fucked him. Used him for my pleasure. And the more I got out of it, the more he did, for I lost myself in the feel of him, giving over to the pleasure, racing for it. I came on a scream that echoed through the forest and as I milked his cock, I felt it swell within me just before he came.

In this moment, both of us lost to the pleasure we could only find in each other, I knew; Quinn and I belonged to each other.

We were one.

EPILOGUE

 uinn, One Month Later, Location Unknown

"Where are we?" I asked, looking around. The transport platform looked as generic and familiar as every other one in the universe.

Five minutes ago, I'd walked into Niobe's office to escort her back to our house. I didn't have to do it; she could make it across the Academy grounds without my escort. I just wanted to be close to her. Being with her made me happy, content in a way I'd never felt before. The restlessness I'd been plagued with my entire life had settled as soon as I'd made *her* my focus. My purpose.

And as soon as I'd insisted Prime Nial get his Coalition protocols and rules out of my fucking way so I could protect my mate.

Instead of gathering her things, as she normally did,

she came around the desk, placed a transport beacon on my chest, took my hand and we were gone.

Transported. Sent... here.

The transport tech behind the panel straightened, saluted. "Vice Admiral," he said. He stared wide-eyed at her as if our arrival was a surprise but said nothing more.

Niobe dropped my hand and went down the steps from the platform. She expected me to follow. Damned straight, I would. Anywhere.

She didn't say a word to the tech, just exited the room and turned right down a long hallway. Everything was nondescript, not giving me any idea where we were. And she'd never answered my question.

Her pace was brisk and efficient and she seemed to know exactly where she was going. Several fighters passed us, saluting as they went.

After a few lefts and rights down corridors, she put her hand up to a panel beside a door. The light turned green and the door slid silently open. Passing through, we were in another hallway, but the temperature was several degrees cooler. Doors lined both sides and she stopped at the third one down on the right.

She faced me for the first time since our arrival and removed the transport beacon from my chest. "You have five minutes, Elite Hunter Quinn."

I frowned, looked at the door. I was no longer referred to by my former title. I was Lieutenant Quinn of the Coalition Fleet now. What game was she playing?

"Five minutes? For what?"

She tipped her chin up, her dark gaze lifting to mine. "Justice."

Her hand slapped against the entry pad beside the door. It beeped, turned green and slid open.

I looked inside and I froze.

The Nexus unit.

I looked at her, making sure I understood.

"They've been at him for over a month. That's long enough. He's yours now."

Holy. Fucking. Shit. This was an I.C. base. Somewhere. And this was a prison area deep within it where the Nexus was housed. I had no doubt there was some kind of lab nearby. I hated the feel of the space, the confinement, knowing there was no escape except through the one door. I'd been within a cell not that different from this one recently, the guest of this blue fucker, and was shocked to realize I was not happy to be here, despite what my mate was offering. I'd tried to find a way to escape my cell, and I'd failed. There was no way out. Not back on Latiri 4 for me, and not here, now, for the blue asshole.

Turning my head, I took him in. He was cut, everywhere, but a thousand tiny slices appeared on his head as if the I.C. scientist had taken a special interest in that region, no doubt trying to figure out how they controlled the minds of the fighters and civilians they integrated. He was thinner, if that was possible. I had assumed he was all machine, but perhaps the biological part of his body had gone hungry. He was naked and I couldn't help but stare at his patchwork of blue and silver pieces. He had ribs, as I did. Arms. Legs. But his dark blue torso was covered in twisting silver, his cock a strange, writhing thing that seemed to have a life of its own. And his dark, black eyes focused on me clearly, despite his weakened state.

"Here to finish me, Hunter?" The Nexus did not smile, nor did he appear to fear my response. And what was my response?

I looked him over and felt... nothing. I had no interest in lingering. I thought of the forest on Zioria, of chasing my mate through the open spaces, the humid air, the rugged terrain. The *freedom*.

I whipped my gaze to Niobe but she had on her vice admiral's expression. Devoid of any emotion. In complete control. This was her doing, her choice. With her rank, access was easy. Even high-level access to personal transport beacons was within her reach.

Fuck.

She'd brought me to the Nexus unit for me to kill it. To finish it, like I'd wanted to when we'd captured it on Latiri 4. She'd refused to give in then, had stood her ground when not one, but several fighters had wanted to kill the Nexus, in direct opposition of her orders. She hadn't given in then. Why was she giving in now?

Because I had. Because I had surrendered to her just as completely as she'd surrendered to me. Not during sex, but in life. In choosing her and the Coalition over my freedom as an Elite Hunter.

I felt cut open. Flayed wide. My heart beating outside of my chest. For this female. How had I been so lucky to be matched to her? She didn't need me. Gods, she was smart, skilled, ruthless, cunning, in control of herself and everything around her. She was brave and had balls bigger than most males.

And she was mine.

I wanted to grab my mate, pull her into my arms and hug her. Kiss the hell out of her. Push her against the wall and fuck her long and hard. She was giving me what I'd wanted. What I thought I'd needed all along. Vengeance for my dead friends. Closure.

"Five minutes," she repeated, glancing at the comm on her wrist.

Time I wouldn't waste. I turned, stepped into the room. The door slid closed behind me. Without looking, I knew Niobe was not within. She waited in the corridor for me to have my time alone with the Nexus unit. To kill him, if that's what I wished.

The Nexus unit was chained as I had been. He could not reach me if he tried.

We stared at one another and I felt the buzzing in my mind, the effect of his nearness on the microscopic integrations that remained in my body. I would never be completely free of him. Not even if I killed him. But he no longer had any influence over me. None.

Our gazes met, and although I felt a strange pull, one thought of Niobe and I had no trouble resisting his psychic influence.

"Nothing to say, Hunter?"

"I'm sorry."

I'd never seen a Nexus unit before this one, and had never seen any emotion on his face during my captivity. But now, I saw surprise. "You apologize? Why?"

Taking a quick inventory of his shackles, his bruises and his lost weight, I knew he'd been through hell, just as I had been. "Because I'm not like you. I am not evil. I do not enjoy watching others suffer, even when they are an enemy."

He blinked, the slow movement of his eyelids over the large, opaque disks strange to witness. "I am not evil. Evil does not exist. Good does not exist. Good. Evil. They are both nothing more than concepts for small minds."

What the fuck was this thing talking about? And why was I talking to him at all?

No. I knew the answer to that question. Curiosity. A need to understand the enemy. "Then why fight this war? Why kill so many of our people?"

The Nexus tilted his head, as if confused. "War? We are not at war. We wish to learn and you resist."

Learn? Was that what he called it? Taking good fighters and turning them into robots? Controlling their minds? Forcing them to kill their friends? Their families? Sometimes their own children?

"Why do you resist?"

"Because we choose to be individuals. We choose freedom."

"Freedom is an illusion. Individuality is an illusion. This body, your body, both an illusion. You are already part of us."

"No. We're not. And we never will be." He would never understand. My head understood that, even though my heart did not. How many buzzing minds did he share? How many integrated fighters' thoughts did he hear? Was he ever alone in his own head? Had he *ever been alone?*

"The future is inevitable, Hunter. You will see. In the end, we are all one."

Fuck that nonsense. As I waited to feel the urge to rip the head from his body, to set my ion pistol to the highest setting and finish him, I realized I didn't want to. Not anymore.

My need to kill it had been so great I'd been blinded, even when Niobe had explained, spoken the truth. The Nexus unit was needed alive. My moment of justice for what he'd done to me was not important enough to supersede the victory that would be achieved by learning from the study of our enemy. Many lives could be saved if the Coalition could gain an understanding of how the Nexus unit worked. How it functioned. How it *thought*. By killing it, that data, that insight, would be lost.

And for what? My personal, petty need to destroy the one small piece of the Hive that had harmed me.

This was war, a war that had been going on for hundreds of years. I'd survived. Others had not. Even more wouldn't if we didn't make deliberate choices and study that which we hated.

If I hadn't been captured, then Niobe wouldn't have transported to me on Latiri 4. She wouldn't have saved me or locked down the underground base. We would not have been able to save all the others or deliver a fucking Nexus unit to the I.C. Alive.

Because I'd been a prisoner, my integrations, my sacrifice, had allowed everything else to fall into place. Had my ultimate purpose as an Elite Hunter been to be captured? To be tortured and matched and saved and brought to this moment so that many millions more could be kept from a similar fate?

If I killed the fucker, my imprisonment would have been for nothing. The imprisonment of the others, their *deaths,* would have been—would *be*—for nothing.

No, it needed to remain alive, just as Niobe had said. The capture and study of the Nexus unit needed to be a victory for the Coalition, a reason for hope in this war.

It wasn't about me. It wasn't about her.

It was about good versus evil. Saving others.

I stepped back, slapped my hand on the wall and took one last look at the blue Nexus unit who now meant nothing to me.

He taunted me with words. "You will learn, Hunter. In the end, you will learn."

His stoic finality was like an ion blast but the shot reflected off my mental armor.

It did not hit. Did not wound. Niobe had healed me, made me stronger. Stronger than the Nexus in this cell. Stronger than my past mistakes. Stronger than I had any right to be, but I would never stop fighting. Never give in. Never stop protecting what was mine. My life. My world. My mate. She was the universe now. My universe. And if Doctor Helion needed to torture and dissect the Nexus unit to help me protect her, so be it.

I turned on my heel and exited the cell. Niobe frowned the moment she saw me leave and spotted the still breathing enemy behind me chained to the wall.

The door slid closed and she stood close, looked into my eyes. "Why?"

I knew the depth of her question.

I stepped closer still, so our bodies brushed. The cell door sealed, the lock making a very distinct sound as my past echoed behind me and enclosed the Nexus unit within, where he would remain to be tested, analyzed. *Used.*

"Because he is the past. You, mate, are my future."

I leaned forward, brushed my lips over hers.

She didn't kiss me back, remained still. Perhaps I'd

stunned her. Confused her with my reversal on the blue fucker.

"You're sure?"

I nodded once, took her hand in mine.

"Positive. I am content to be yours. Your security. Your protection. Your mate. Just yours, Niobe."

Her brow arched, studied me, perhaps to see if I spoke the truth, if I meant the words. She nodded, seemingly appeased.

She led me back toward the transport room, but glanced over at me.

"I love you, you know that?"

I smiled and tugged on her arm, kissed her again, because I could, because she was mine. "I know. I love you more."

She raised a brow, the vice admiral's cold, calculating assessment of my words apparent on her face... until she grinned up at me like a goddess who'd just been given a gift—and I realized that *gift* was me. I would care for her, protect her, love her, dedicate the rest of my life to making her happy and I couldn't wait to get started.

We walked in silence after that until we stood upon the transport pad once again. "Return transport. Reverse coordinates," she ordered the transport tech.

"Ready, mate?" she asked, the heat and sizzle of the imminent transport raising the hair on my arms.

"With you? Always."

Ready for more? Read Viken Command next!

Whitney Mason is the daughter of a Wall Street con man. When he is sent to prison and her family's name is destroyed, she is eager for a new life on a new world. Anywhere but Earth. Tested by the Interstellar Brides Program, she is matched to a strong Viken warrior. What she doesn't know is that her mate and the other two warriors waiting to claim her are on a secret and dangerous mission for the Coalition Fleet's Intelligence Core. From the moment she arrives on Viken, they are forced to lie to her... about everything... except their desire.

For Alarr, Oran and Teig, the arrival of a bride is an unexpected complication. The timing couldn't be worse, but IC command is thrilled. A bride is the perfect cover, giving the fighters access to every inch of the famous pleasure resort where they are working undercover. The males are eager to satisfy their new mate, but keeping her safe is their top priority, even if that means lying to her and using her pleasure to take down the enemy. But their sexy mate's past will come back to haunt them all, for even if they survive the mission, the truth will be revealed and their beautiful, curvy female can forgive anything— except lies.

Click here to get Viken Command now!

A SPECIAL THANK YOU TO MY READERS...

Want more? I've got *hidden* bonus content on my web site *exclusively* for those on my mailing list.

If you are already on my email list, you don't need to do a thing! Simply scroll to the bottom of my newsletter emails and click on the *super-secret* link.

Not a member? What are you waiting for? In addition to ALL of my bonus content (great new stuff will be added regularly) you will be the first to hear about my newest release the second it hits the stores—AND you will get a free book as a special welcome gift.

Sign up now! http://freescifiromance.com

FIND YOUR INTERSTELLAR MATCH!

YOUR mate is out there. Take the test today and discover your perfect match. Are you ready for a sexy alien mate (or two)?

VOLUNTEER NOW!

interstellarbridesprogram.com

DO YOU LOVE AUDIOBOOKS?

Grace Goodwin's books are now available as audiobooks...everywhere.

LET'S TALK SPOILER ROOM!

Interested in joining my **Sci-Fi Squad**? Meet new like-minded sci-fi romance fanatics and chat with Grace! Get excerpts, cover reveals and sneak peeks before anyone else. Be part of a private Facebook group that shares pictures and fun news! Join here:

https://www.facebook.com/groups/scifisquad/

***

Want to talk about Grace Goodwin books with others? Join the **SPOILER ROOM** and spoil away! Your GG BFFs are waiting! (And so is Grace)

Join here:

https://www.facebook.com/groups/ggspoilerroom/

GET A FREE BOOK!

JOIN MY MAILING LIST TO BE THE FIRST TO KNOW OF NEW RELEASES, FREE BOOKS, SPECIAL PRICES AND OTHER AUTHOR GIVEAWAYS.

http://freescifiromance.com

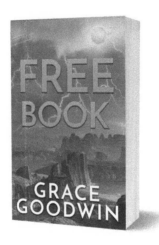

ALSO BY GRACE GOODWIN

Interstellar Brides® Program

Assigned a Mate

Mated to the Warriors

Claimed by Her Mates

Taken by Her Mates

Mated to the Beast

Mastered by Her Mates

Tamed by the Beast

Mated to the Vikens

Her Mate's Secret Baby

Mating Fever

Her Viken Mates

Fighting For Their Mate

Her Rogue Mates

Claimed By The Vikens

The Commanders' Mate

Matched and Mated

Hunted

Viken Command

The Rebel and the Rogue

Interstellar Brides® Program: The Colony

Surrender to the Cyborgs

Mated to the Cyborgs

Cyborg Seduction

Her Cyborg Beast

Cyborg Fever

Rogue Cyborg

Cyborg's Secret Baby

Her Cyborg Warriors

Interstellar Brides® Program: The Virgins

The Alien's Mate

His Virgin Mate

Claiming His Virgin

His Virgin Bride

His Virgin Princess

Interstellar Brides® Program: Ascension Saga

Ascension Saga, book 1

Ascension Saga, book 2

Ascension Saga, book 3

Trinity: Ascension Saga - Volume 1

Ascension Saga, book 4

Ascension Saga, book 5

Ascension Saga, book 6

Faith: Ascension Saga - Volume 2

Ascension Saga, book 7

Ascension Saga, book 8

Ascension Saga, book 9

Destiny: Ascension Saga - Volume 3

Other Books

Their Conquered Bride

Wild Wolf Claiming: A Howl's Romance

ABOUT GRACE

Grace Goodwin is a USA Today and international bestselling author of Sci-Fi and Paranormal romance with more than one million books sold. Grace's titles are available worldwide in multiple languages in ebook, print and audio formats. Two best friends, one left-brained, the other right-brained, make up the award-winning writing duo that is Grace Goodwin.

They are both mothers, escape room enthusiasts, avid readers and intrepid defenders of their preferred beverages. (There may or may not be an ongoing tea vs. coffee war occurring during their daily communications.) Grace loves to hear from readers!

All of Grace's books can be read as sexy, stand-alone adventures. But be careful, she likes her heroes hot and her love scenes hotter. You have been warned...

www.gracegoodwin.com
gracegoodwinauthor@gmail.com